# diary of a 6th grade ninja 10

## my worst frenemy

### BY MARCUS EMERSON
AND NOAH CHILD

ILLUSTRATED BY DAVID LEE

EMERSON PUBLISHING HOUSE

## ALSO BY MARCUS EMERSON

*The Diary of a 6th Grade Ninja Series*
*Diary of a 6th Grade Ninja*
*Pirate Invasion*
*Rise of the Red Ninjas*
*A Game of Chase*
*Terror at the Talent Show*
*Buchanan Bandits*
*Scavengers*
*Spirit Week Shenanigans*
*The Scavengers Strike Back*

*The Secret Agent 6th Grader Series*
*Secret Agent 6th Grader*
*Ice Cold Suckerpunch*
*Extra Large Soda Jerk*
*Selfies are Forever*

*Totes Sweet Hero*

# MY WORST FRENEMY

Here's a bit of advice for anyone out there who'd like to be an evil villain someday— if your phone rings, *answer* it. How can you make insane demands and then *ignore* all your phone calls?

That's what Vesh was doing… and that's why Naoki and I were scaling a building using nothing but a thin rope. You ever climb a building with a thin rope? I don't recommend it.

Wait.

Let me start again so things make more sense.

Naoki and I were walking up the side of a hundred-story building. At the top was one of the most notorious criminals our galaxy had ever seen. We weren't sure whether he was expecting us or not, but I guess we were about to find out.

Vesh had taken the Earth hostage, threatening to use his ultra powerful planet-eating machine on the planet unless he was paid a duodecillion fossil credits. You know how many zeroes are in a duodecillion?

*Thirty-nine.*

That's 1,000,000,000,000,000,000,000,000,000,000,000,000,000.

I guess it's a good thing he didn't ask for *two* duodecillion fossil credits, right?

The people of Earth tried to contact Vesh several times in hopes of working out a deal that didn't end with the destruction of the planet, because, y'know... that kind of thing could really ruin someone's day.

But Vesh never answered a single phone call.

I know, right? What kind of alien monster carries around a chintzy cell phone to begin with? Bad guys need better tech than that. Total noob.

The thing about Vesh's cell was that he was clearly *ignoring* the phone calls. It wasn't that the calls weren't going through, and it wasn't that his phone was out of earshot. The call would ring twice, and then go straight to voicemail. That dude was clicking the ignore button... but why?

Oh, and the text messages that Earthlings sent to him were delivered – there wasn't any doubt about that because Vesh forgot to change his phone settings, which meant his cell phone would send a "read receipt" back to the other phone that text him.

You can't imagine how frustrating that was!

*C'mon, Vesh! Be a better villain!*

So... that's when yours truly was called upon to save the day once again.

My name is Chase Cooper, and I'm a sixth grade ninja... climbing up the side of a building to meet with an alien who has high anxiety about answering phone calls.

Naoki, my trusty raccoon sidekick, was ahead of me, scratching his little paws against the side of the building, walking himself up the wall. His backpack hung from his shoulder and dangled above my face.

"You mind strapping your bag tighter?" I said, a little annoyed at the swinging canvas sack that kept brushing the tip of my nose.

"Sorry, master," Naoki said. "If I had an extra paw right now, I'd totally do it, but I fear I might fall."

"Right," I said. "Just concentrate on climbing."

"If Vesh would've just answered his stinkin' phone, we wouldn't have to do any of this!" Naoki said. "And what're all these demands for fossil credits? If he woulda answered his phone, then maybe he'd know nobody has a clue what a fossil credit is! It'd be like demanding a bajillion unicorn horns! It doesn't make any sense!"

I laughed at my partner's frustration. Naoki's mouth ran

like a river when he was upset. "Dude," I said. "It'll all work out in the end. All we have to do is get to the top of the building, and try talking some sense into the sociopathic evil alien who wants to destroy the planet."

Naoki was about to respond, but a loudspeaker cackled from somewhere in the sky.

"Attention, citizens of Earth," said the voice. It was a deep, dark voice that sounded reptilian. "Due to your failure to pay me, your planet will be devoured in just a few short minutes. Um... sorry 'bout that."

"We must hurry, master!" Naoki said, taking larger steps against the side of the building.

I clutched the rope tighter, pulling myself up as fast as I could.

Right at that moment, one of the windows in the side of the building slid open. I flinched, thinking Vesh had sent down a bunch of spiders or something to stop me from getting to him, but when I saw who opened the window, I *wished* it had only been a bunch of spiders.

It was Wyatt, and he had a determined "*I'm here to*

*help*" look in his eye.

"S'up, guys?" Wyatt said, leaning his head way out the window. "Whatcha doin' out here?"

Naoki groaned. "What's it look like? *We're tryin' t'save the world!*"

"Yeah," I said. "Little busy right now."

"It's cool," Wyatt said, scooting his butt across the windowsill until he grabbed onto the rope Naoki and I were climbing up. "I'll help!"

"No, no," I said. The rope tightened as Wyatt hopped from the window and hung below me. "We're good, man! We don't need any help!"

"Yep, ya do!" Wyatt said. "Be like water, bro!"

"*What?*" I said.

Naoki spoke from above. "He said 'be like water.' Water has no shape, but will take the shape of any container. It flows, transforms, and adapts to its surroundings, no matter what they are."

"There it is," Wyatt said. "I'm here, and now I'm helping. *Deal with it!*"

"Master," Naoki whispered. "We haven't the time for this. Just let him tag along for now. Vesh is only *minutes* away from destroying the world!"

I nodded at my raccoon sidekick. Looking down, I was *going* to tell Wyatt that if he wanted to help, he had to be careful, but I wasn't even able to get the words out.

Wyatt grabbed the bottom of my jeans and pulled himself up. He climbed right on top of my back and kept moving upward like it was a race.

"So how'd you guys get this gig?" Wyatt asked as he rudely planted his feet on my shoulders to boost himself higher. "Do you freelance your ninja services or something?"

"Freelance?" Naoki repeated.

"Yeah," Wyatt said, and then explained. "Freelancing is when you're working for yourself, finding jobs and stuff to pay the bills. So, like, do you two go around finding random jobs like this and then get paid for going on the adventure?"

"Random jobs," Naoki whispered sarcastically. "Like saving the Earth from total destruction…"

"Of course not!" I said. "There's no paycheck for us! We're doing this because our *planet* is being threatened by an alien monster!"

"Huh," Wyatt grunted, unimpressed. "Then you lamewads are bad at business, which... is good for me. Since I don't have a ninja clan anymore, I'm looking to branch out on my own, y'know? I wanna do the stuff you're doing, but do it *better* and get paid for it."

Wyatt grabbed Naoki's tail and swung back and forth. Naoki squealed like a baby chicken... or, I guess a baby raccoon would make more sense, since, y'know... that's what Naoki was.

"Let go of my tail or feel the wrath of my ancestors!" Naoki growled.

"Look at me, guys!" Wyatt squealed, swinging by Naoki's furry tail. "I'm a monkey!"

"Wyatt!" I said, feeling like a frustrated parent. "Let go of his tail this instant! You're rockin' the rope too much! We're gonna fall if you don't stop acting like a child!"

Planting both feet on the side of the building, Wyatt stopped swinging. And then he stuck out his tongue and blew a raspberry at me.

"Seriously?" I said way louder than I meant to.

From the top of the building, a silver robotic eye peeked over the edge and spotted us. It must've been one of Vesh's cameras because it suddenly flashed red, and an alarm thundered through the entire building.

"Great," I said. "So much for our surprise attack."

Naoki gasped. "Master, look out! Tiny robotic ninjas are falling from the rooftop!"

"Tiny robotic ninjas?" Wyatt said. "Flippin' sweet!"

The ninjas fell all around us like rain. Several of them landed squarely on our shoulders and started ninja kicking us. You'd think tiny robot ninjas attacking you would kind of tickle, but I'm here to tell you it *doesn't* tickle... it hurts.

Wyatt's attitude quickly shifted from delight to sheer terror as soon as the small ninjas started attacking.

"Get 'em off a me!" Wyatt screeched. "They're punching me with their tiny fists!"

"They're punching *all* of us with their tiny fists!" Naoki said.

Flailing wildly, Wyatt did the dumbest thing a person could do while climbing a building with a thin rope – he let go.

Naoki shouted as Wyatt fell on top of him. Naoki was a strong raccoon, but when someone three times your size body

5

slams you from above, it doesn't matter how tightly you're holding a rope – you're gonna fall.

And then there was me at the bottom, staring helplessly as a raccoon and an eleven-year-old boy came crashing down on top of me.

I squeezed the rope in my hands, but that just burned as I slid down a couple feet. Finally, letting go, I arched myself back, reaching my hands out to grab the nearest windowsill, but they were all too far away. The whole building was too far away as Naoki, Wyatt, and I fell into a free-fall.

The air was brisk, and bit my cheeks through my ninja mask as I fell faster and faster. The world spun circles around me, or rather, I was spinning uncontrollably, which made it *look* like the world was spinning circles.

The tiny robot ninjas flaked off my shoulders. The fall must've been too much for them to handle. They got their job done and were probably headed back to Vesh who was still on the roof.

Was that it? Was that the way the world was going to end? What were the history books going to say about it, I wondered. Then I realized there wouldn't *be* any history books written about it… ever.

Wyatt was hollering something from somewhere I couldn't see. All I could hear was the air blasting past my ears and Wyatt's annoying voice. He sounded like he was having fun!

And then there came another sound, like an explosion, and close. A little *too* close.

A tiny raccoon hand grabbed the bottom of my jeans and stopped me from spinning like a violent ballerina.

"Hang on, master!" Naoki shouted as he tightened his grip on me. In the raccoon's other hand was Wyatt who was freaking out.

On Naoki's back was a jetpack, blasting fire from

beneath it. The backpack my sidekick had been wearing was actually a jetpack!

Wait… the backpack my sidekick had been wearing was actually a jetpack?

*"You had a jetpack the whole time?"* I shouted over the noise of the rockets shooting off behind Naoki. *"Why didn't you use that thing to begin with? We could've skipped the whole 'climbing the side of the building with cheap rope' thing!"*

"I never said anything because you never asked, master!" Naoki replied.

"I shouldn't have to ask about something like that!" I said. "Okay, from now on, if you have a tool that'll help *any* of our missions, just tell me from the start!"

Naoki smiled. "Understood!"

The three of us rocketed to the top of the building, where Vesh was working on his planet-eating machine. He was hunched over a spot at the foot of the machine as sparks danced around him.

Naoki released Wyatt and me. We both fell to the top of the roof, landing gracefully. Naoki shut down his jetpack and dropped between us.

As if Vesh could *feel* our presence, he stopped his work on the machine, and stood to his feet. The Earth's atmosphere was too much for the alien, because he was still wearing his space helmet that was shaped like a ball.

The alien monster was at least ten feet tall. He arched his back, stretching it out like he had just come home from a long day at work. Slowly, like in a creepy horror movie, he turned around until he was completely facing us.

That's when I realized his body wasn't what I thought it was. It was just a robotic shell that was controlled by a tiny little alien sitting inside the helmet on top.

Vesh was an itty bitty little thing. If he weren't about to destroy the world, I would've said he was kind of cute. He was even wearing a tiny t-shirt!

The alien clapped his hands slowly, like he was applauding. "Well, well, well," he said from inside the glass helmet. "If it isn't Charley Cooper."

"It's *Chase*," I said, correcting him. "My name's Chase, dude."

"Charley, Chase, it doesn't make a lick of difference,

does it?" Vesh said, holding one of his hands out, presenting the machine that was behind him. "In a few short minutes, your planet will be *toooooooast*, and *nobody* will remember you."

"Why haven't you answered your phone?" Naoki huffed.

Vesh shrugged his tiny shoulders. "I'unno," he muttered. "I prefer texting."

"But people texted you too!" Naoki added.

Vesh's face hinted that he wanted to smile. "I'm not too good with new technology." He held his giganto robot hands in front of his face. "I got these fat fingers and those buttons are super tiny."

"So that's why our planet is going to be destroyed?" Wyatt replied. "*Because of your giant sausage fingers?*"

"Dude, easy," Naoki said.

"Oh, I'm sorry," Wyatt said sarcastically. "We wouldn't

want to hurt his feelings, right?"

"You don't wanna set off the dude who wants to blow up the planet," I said. "You gotta be more careful about how you approach—"

Wyatt leaned his head back and groaned. "You buncha dandelions! Watch how a *pro* does this," he said, marching forward.

"What're you doing?" I whispered harshly. "Just hang back! I got this under control!"

Wyatt spun around with his arms outstretched. "Really? This is 'under control' to you?"

"I mean," I said, stumbling over my tongue. "I was *about* to talk him out of it!"

"You were going to *negotiate?*" Wyatt said. "Forget that! While you negotiate with your mouth from *way* back there, I'll go right up to him and negotiate with my *fists!*"

With that, Wyatt turned and sprinted straight for the ten-foot-tall robot shell that contained Vesh.

Wyatt flipped over, somehow instantly changing into his red ninja outfit. Honestly, if the planet weren't in danger of being eaten, I probably would've thought his "quick-change" stunt was pretty cool.

Vesh planted one foot back. At first, it looked like he was bracing himself for Wyatt's attack, but it was quickly obvious that he didn't care about whatever Wyatt was trying to do. Instead, the alien set his hands on the planet-eating machine and brought up a holographic control panel.

Screaming like a crazy cat lady, Wyatt flew through the air, throwing out a bicycle kick that would make any kung fu master LOL. It actually looked like Wyatt was riding an invisible bicycle.

"What move is that?" Naoki asked.

"Not one from any book *I've* ever read," I said.

Sadly, Wyatt's move failed on a level so epic that even *I* felt embarrassed for him. His bicycle kick landed directly on Vesh's back, but... have you ever hit a tiny rock while skateboarding? It doesn't matter how fast you're going, once your skateboard wheel hits that rock, you fall flat to the ground like a ragdoll. You could be coasting at a hundred miles an hour, and then *BA-BAM!* You face plant into the ground so hard that it made people on the other side of the world cringe.

Wyatt's bicycle kick did nothing when he made contact

with Vesh's back. Instead of some awesome finishing move, Wyatt plopped to the ground and screamed in pain.

Vesh didn't even flinch. He continued to play with the holographic display in front of him, twisting and turning various circles until finding what he was looking for.

Finally, the alien put his hand directly into the middle of a blue holographic sphere, clutched his fist like he was grabbing something inside of it, and turned his wrist.

The planet-eating machine came to life on top of the building. The sound was so loud that I couldn't hear anything else but the grinding noise it made.

Naoki covered his ears and shouted at me, but no words were coming from his mouth. I had to read his lips in order to understand him.

*"You have to stop the machine! We have to switch it off somehow?"* he said.

I mouthed back to my raccoon sidekick, *"But how? I don't know anything about that thing, do you?"*

Naoki shook his head.

I looked at the city streets below us. The planet-eating machine was working. I knew because even from way up high, I could see the concrete cracking and splitting apart. Cars and buses were thrown back and forth like toys.

Naoki tugged at my jeans, pointing back at Vesh's planet eating machine.

When I saw what Naoki was pointing at, I felt pretty dumb that I didn't see it earlier. There, at the side of the monstrous machine, was a giant plug hooked up to an oversized socket on the rooftop. It looked like something from a cartoon.

"For real?" I said to Naoki, but my raccoon sidekick couldn't hear me.

Running for the plug, I saw Vesh turn to face me, but I was too quick for him. I grabbed the thick wire around the plug and yanked back as hard as I could. Lucky for me, and the rest of the planet, the plug slipped right out.

The cars bouncing around on the city streets crashed to the concrete as Earth's gravity returned to normal.

"You fool!" Vesh screamed from his glass helmet. "You've only delayed the inevitable! I'll return to your pathetic planet and finish the job later!"

"Not if I stop you first!" I shouted. My ears were still

ringing from the noise Vesh's machine made… was *still* making.

Vesh's machine was still surging with power!

The alien monster lifted his fist and pointed it at the floor around him. A burst of green light came from his forearm, creating a swirling portal back to his home world.

"How can you stop me when you're too busy saving yourself?" Vesh growled. And then he stepped into the portal. The gateway collapsed once he was all the way through.

"The machine!" Naoki shouted. "It's gonna blow!"

Naoki was right. Vesh's machine had become unstable, shaking the building violently. Little pebbles danced around our feet.

"We have to switch it off!" I said.

"But you *unplugged* it!" Naoki said. "What else is there to do?"

I looked at the plug, which was on the ground. The gears glowed red as flames shot from the top of the device.

"Nothing is ever as easy as it seems!" Wyatt shouted from behind.

I spun around in time to see Wyatt yank Naoki's jetpack off his tiny raccoon body. Every muscle in my body burned as I started running after the kid.

"Wait!" I said as Wyatt ran to the edge of the building. He pulled the jetpack over his arms as I pleaded with him. "That thing can carry all three of us! We can *all* escape if you'd just wait one second!"

Wyatt leapt from the roof, spinning to face me. "Too late, losers!"

My feet dug into the ground, and I slid to a stop inches away from the edge. The little pebbles at my feet slipped over the side, falling to the street below, which, BTW, was about a hundred floors down.

Naoki's voice came from behind. "Jump!" he shouted.

Right when I turned around, Naoki hopped onto my chest, pushing me off the ledge. At that exact moment, Vesh's machine exploded, rattling the entire building. Glass windows on the upper floors shattered from the tremors.

The heat from the blast was so intense that I could feel the warmth even from the side of the building where Naoki and I were falling for a second time.

The rush of air screamed in my ears as I tried to steady myself. We were only seconds away from hitting the pavement. I had to think of something quick.

And then I heard Wyatt's laughter. He was floating in place high in the sky, watching Naoki and me fall from the building.

Naoki gripped the sides of my head and shook it. "Pay attention, man! You gotta think of something!"

I stuttered, but I don't know what I said. It was like my brain was totally wiped clean. I opened my mouth to talk, but the only thing that came out... was a scream.

**Monday. 7:35 AM. My locker.**

"Whooooa, Chase!" Brayden said like I was a horse he was trying to stop.

I was on the floor in front of my locker, coughing from the scream I had just let out. I could hear students giggling at me from somewhere in the hall.

There, standing in front of me, was my cousin Zoe, and my best friend Brayden… and they looked upset.

Brayden looked embarrassed for me, keeping his eyes turned to the ground. It was probably because everyone in the entire school heard my scream.

Zoe was next to him. She held her hands against her chest as if she had just been frightened. "Dude, what's the matter with you?"

I froze, blinking as I waited for Vesh to burst through the crowd. I don't know why, but for some reason I wasn't convinced that was the real world.

"This is it, isn't it?" Zoe asked. "This is the moment I'm going to remember as the moment my cousin snapped. When I tell my kids about their uncle in the loony bin, the story will start with this *exact* second. He just went nuts in the middle of school. He had no way to control the volume of his voice…

14

always screaming instead of talking."
    I swallowed hard, looking around.

    Other students whispered loud enough that I could hear
them.
    *"What a weirdo."*
    *"Sleeping in the hallway is such a lazy-kid thing to do."*
    *"He should've stayed at his old school. Ever since he
got here, there's been nothing but trouble."*
    My face felt warm, and I had that feeling in my stomach
– the one I got whenever I felt stupid.
    "Am I still dreaming?" I asked as I pushed my back
against my locker to help me stand.
    "Ah," Zoe said. "You screamed because of a dream,
which… is *still* a red flag for someone going crazy, y'know?
Nightmares in the middle of school and all that."
    I wiped the sleep from my eyes and pulled my cheeks
down to stretch my face. I was still groggy. "I mean, is this
real now?"
    "Nice," Brayden said. "What if this is a dream *inside* a
dream? Do you know what *that* would mean?"

"No," I said. "What would it mean?"

Brayden shrugged and shook his head. "Oh, I don't know either. That's why I asked."

I've known Brayden since the first week of school at Buchanan. We've had our rough patches, but every friendship does. My dad says it's what turns "kind of friends" into "best friends." I'm not gonna argue with my dad. He seems to know what he's talking about… *most* of the time.

I felt a sting on my forearm. Zoe's fingers were pinched around the skin above my wrist. It seriously felt like she poked me with a flaming hot needle.

"Ouch!" I yelped, pulling my arm away from my cousin. Zoe had a smile. She didn't say anything.

Zoe was one of my cousins. She was the only cousin who went to Buchanan School. The rest were at Armstrong School, halfway across town. Armstrong was actually where I transferred from. Bryce and Al, my two other cousins were still students at Armstrong. I only transferred because my family moved into another district.

"You're supposed to pinch *yourself* to wake up," Brayden said to Zoe.

"Yeah!" I said, rubbing the burn on my arm. "I was supposed to pinch *myself!*"

Zoe pinched a spot on my other arm.

"*Would you stop that?*" I shouted in pain.

Zoe smiled. "I guess you're not dreaming anymore."

I folded my arms across my chest, rubbing both spots my cousin pinched. I couldn't pinch anyone like that if I practiced it a thousand times. What is it about girls just *knowing* how to inflict *that* much pain with only two fingers?

Brayden unzipped his book bag and took out a small black glass bottle, about the size of trading card. He popped off the cap, held it to his neck, and sprayed whatever was inside onto his skin.

"Cologne, huh?" I said. "The men's perfume."

"Hey, dude," Brayden said slyly, posing like he was in a magazine ad. "Ladies dig a kid who *smells* like a man."

"You smell like a pine tree," Zoe said, waving her hands in front of her body to try and keep the cologne from wafting over to her. "Great, your pine tree mist is all over my shirt! Now *I* smell like a man!"

"Sorry," Brayden said, pushing the cap back onto his

cologne bottle. "But I forgot to spray this on before I left home."

"So your only other option was to do it in a packed hallway?" Zoe said, annoyed and still waving her hands in front of her. "You should've gone to the locker room!"

"I did!" Brayden said. "I sprayed it there first... and now I'm spraying here."

Zoe dropped her arms, shocked. "*Once. Once* is enough for that junk!"

"Okaaaay," Brayden said, raising his eyebrows and bobbing his head back and forth.

I glanced back and forth down the hallway, watching all the other students walk with their friends.

"Why were you napping in front of your locker?" Zoe asked.

"I was waiting for Naomi," I said. "We were going to go to that thing in the library together."

For those who don't know, Naomi was another good friend of mine. Brayden and I had our rough patches, but Naomi and I had our burnt bridge that we were trying to rebuild.

I won't go too far into detail, because there's *a lot* of detail. Basically, she betrayed me, pretended to be my friend, tried to destroy my life, came back and apologized, and then sacrificed her own social life to make it up to me. So, yeah... there's a lot of history between us.

"If she was supposed to meet you at your locker," Zoe said, "then why's she late?"

"Maybe she got caught in a hall jam," I said.

"Maybe she's plotting to destroy you," Zoe said, but closed her eyes and shook her head as soon as she said it. "No, no, no. I didn't mean that. It's just... she didn't meet you where you wanted to meet. You sure you can trust her? Not that I'm saying you shouldn't, but y'know... just asking."

Even though Naomi and I were talking again, Zoe had a point, and it's a point that had been on my mind since Naomi apologized.

I nodded at my cousin. "I trust her," I said. "But can we really be sure we can trust anybody?"

"Um, yeah," Zoe said. "I'm pretty sure I know who I can and can't trust."

Brayden straightened his posture and spoke with a much

deeper voice than normal. "Forgiveness is what makes good men great."

"Stop trying to be a man," Zoe sighed.

Brayden smiled. "All I'm sayin' is that it's a good thing Naomi and Chase are friends again."

"She said sorry," I added. "And I believe she was. Isn't that the only thing that matters?"

Zoe nodded. "It is," she said. "You're right. Normally, I'm the one who makes all the mature decisions. It's nice to see you do that for a change."

I made the dorkiest smile I could while giving my cousin two thumbs-up.

She giggled. "Nerd."

"But…" I said, scanning the crowd one last time, "I don't think she's coming here."

"Maybe she got caught up," Brayden said.

I sighed. "Maybe."

Brayden, Zoe, and I made our way through the halls of Buchanan School, to the library where the assembly was going to be held.

This is probably a good time to fill you in on all the stuff that's happened in my crazy life.

It had only been a weekend since the whole thing with Victor went down in the cafeteria.

Victor was the leader of the Scavengers, a group of kids who know the secrets of everyone in the school. They learn these secrets by eavesdropping on your conversation, reading your text messages over your shoulder, and stealing all the notes you wrote to your friends *after* you've thrown them away in the trash.

The Scavengers knew everything. Every tiny little secret you think you're keeping safe in your head; The Scavengers probably know about it.

Victor was the leader of the whole shebang. He was an eighth grader who wore an earing and dressed like he was in a boy band – y'know, two collared shirts, both flipped up, along with baggy pants that looked like something my parents used to wear in high school. He had glasses too, but I doubted they were even real.

Victor planned on destroying more of my life, but thanks to Naomi, he didn't get away with it.

The last time I saw Victor, a couple kids in suits and

18

sunglasses were escorting him out of the cafeteria. It was kind of weird… like he was being taken away by a couple secret agents or something.

Previously on... diary of a 6th grade ninja

Scavengers + Victor = Horrible

Wyatt − Red ninjas = Less Horrible

Red ninjas + Green ninjas = Holiday Ninjas?

The Scavengers hadn't said a word to me since Victor was taken away, but that didn't mean they weren't around. I'd bet my whole comic book collection that I haven't seen the last of them.

Well, not my *whole* comic book collection. I spent a lot of time searching for certain variant covers. Those were comin' with me to my grave.

Oh, and on top of dealing with The Scavengers, there was also some trouble with the red ninjas *and* a group of new *green* ninjas.

Wyatt (you remember him from my dream) is the leader of the red ninja clan… or at least, *used* to be the leader of them. His ninja clan had grown so big that they sort of overthrew his leadership. That meant someone *else* had control of the red ninjas, but nobody knew who it was.

It was the same with the green ninja clan that recently sprouted up. I didn't know who the leader of that clan was, and I'm not so sure Wyatt knew either. It was kind of the mystery of the week.

And me? I was just trying to coast through the rest of the school year. I thought it was best to let everything calm down before doing anything else. Dealing with The Scavengers, Victor, Wyatt, and different ninja clans was more than a sixth grader needed on his plate.

I was at the point in my life where being "cool" wasn't even something I thought I wanted anymore. I'd been hated by so many different people for the past couple of months, that honestly, one step above whatever step I was on would've made me happy.

I just didn't want to be hated anymore.

No, I didn't want to be *super* hated anymore.

**Monday. 7:40 AM. The lobby.**

I turned the corner and stopped outside the lobby of the school. Brayden and Zoe were still with me, joking about how all the kids were crammed into the school like a bunch of sardines.

Everyone was waiting to get into the library.

"Zoe, you're president," I said. "Why don't you just push your way through the crowd?"

"Doesn't work like that," Zoe said.

"Oh, right," Brayden said. "You're supposed to have bodyguards and stuff do that for you."

Zoe laughed. "I wish! I wouldn't mind a crew walking me everywhere."

My eyebrows raised. "Hey, you got Brayden and me! We're all the crew you need!"

"My own ninja bodyguards," Zoe said quietly, and then paused. "That's not such a bad idea, but... I think I'd come off as more of a villain if I traveled with ninjas everywhere I went."

"If, by *villain*, you mean *way cool president*," I said, "then yes, you'd be a *way cool president*."

Zoe sighed, pushing up on her tiptoes to see over

21

everyone's head. "C'mon, man. This is taking forever. This crowd's barely moving. Are the doors even open?"

I tried to see past everyone, but the crowd was too thick. "I dunno," I said. "At least everyone's excited to get in there."

"They should be," Zoe said, returning to her normal height by dropping back to her heels. "It wasn't easy to get Dr. Tenderfoot to visit the school. He doesn't really do school visits."

"Tenderfoot," I repeated. "Who's this guy again?"

"Ashley Tenderfoot," Zoe said. She was going to continue, but Brayden cut her off.

"Ashley?" Brayden said, scrunching his nose. He was the one on his tiptoes that time looking over everyone's head. "Dude's first name is Ashley? That's a girl's name."

"Um, it's not," Zoe said, annoyed. "And you better not say anything about it when we're in there. Dr. Tenderfoot is a highly respected pioneer in robotics research. He founded Tenderfoot Industries."

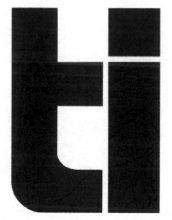

# TENDERFOOT
# INDUSTRIES

I leaned closer to Brayden and whispered, "That means he's supes important."

"He's not *just* supes important," Zoe said. "He's, like, *the* dude everyone talks about when they talk about robot science. His lab is working on some pretty crazy stuff."

"Like 'end of the world' crazy stuff?" I said. "Is he the guy who's going to create the machines that turn against humans someday?"

"Maybe," Zoe said. "But for now, we're probably safe." The doors to the library must've opened because all the kids in the lobby shuffled forward, like zombies in search of their next meal.

"It took a *ton* of emails to get Dr. Tenderfoot to agree to come here for the week," Zoe continued. "And he only did it if we agreed to host a robotics competition for the students in the school."

"Ooooo!" I said, excited. "Like, getting robots to fight each other in the ring?"

"Noooo," Zoe replied. "Like, getting a couple teams of kids to build their own robot."

"And then getting them to fight to the death? Their *robot* death?" Brayden said.

"OMG, no, you guys," Zoe said. "The teams will build their own robot and then, at the end of the week, present them to the school and Dr. Tenderfoot. Best one wins."

"Wins what?" I asked, slightly hopeful that the answer was going to be "a robot sidekick."

"A robot sidekick," Zoe said.

My jaw dropped.

My cousin laughed at me. "I know you too well. The prize *isn't* a robot sidekick. I don't know what it is, but it's not that."

"Oh," I said, kicking a spot on the carpet like a little child. And then I whispered under my breath, "Robot sidekicks are cool."

"So wait," Brayden said as we continued to move forward. "We're sixth graders, and we're expected to *build* a robot? Like it's that easy?"

Zoe shook her head. "No," she said. "Just wait until you get in there. Dr. Tenderfoot will explain the whole thing better than I can."

We continued scraping our feet along the carpet until we were finally at the front doors of the library. I could tell the room was packed because most of the kids in there were standing since there weren't any seats left.

Suddenly, a creepy, dark voice came from behind us.

"Mistah Coooooopah!"

I turned around, but wasn't afraid because I recognized the voice. It was Naomi.

"S'up, dude?" Naomi said, nudging me with her shoulder.

"Hey!" I said, super happy to see my friend.

"You weren't at your locker," Naomi said.

"Oh, but he was," Zoe sighed, making it obvious that she wasn't too happy that Naomi and I were friends again. And I knew it wasn't because she didn't like Naomi – it was that she didn't want to see her cousin get burned again. Zoe's cool like that.

"You were?" Naomi said.

I mumbled some words before finding my voice again. "I sorta fell asleep."

"Dude," Naomi said. "You gotta lay off the late night video games."

"Right?" Zoe said.

"Okay," I said, and then added, "Except we were playing online together last night."

Naomi tried to hide a smile, but couldn't.

Zoe rolled her eyes, but it wasn't mean. It was more like the way an adult would wag their finger at a couple of children and say, *"You kiddos and your video games!"*

"We'll be inside," Zoe said, grabbing Brayden's elbow to pull him along.

"Wait," Brayden said. "I don't wanna go in yet. I'll go in when Chase goes in!"

Zoe gave him a quick look that was like, "C'mon, already."

I'm not sure why Zoe wanted to leave Naomi and me alone. It might've been because she didn't want to say anything to Naomi that she'd regret.

Brayden sighed, and followed my cousin into the library.

The lobby cleared out completely, leaving Naomi and me outside the library doors.

"Finally," Naomi said. "Now that we're alone… my Scavengers will completely *crush* you for good!"

Oh, great. Maybe my cousin was right about Naomi after all.

24

**Monday. 7:45 AM. Outside the library.**

Naomi had just threatened me. I wasn't sure how to respond except with... "Uh... okay?"

She laughed, and then threw her arms around me. "I'm kidding!"

Naomi squeezed me so hard that my throat let out a weird "*quack*" sound.

"Did you quack at me?" Naomi asked, still hugging my body.

"Maybe," I said, embarrassed.

"You know I was joking, right?" Naomi said. "That's how we used to joke with each other, but... too soon?"

I chuckled, feeling relieved. "No, it's cool. I was just a little shocked."

"I know," Naomi said. "You were so shocked that you *quacked* at me."

Pushing open the door to the library, I let Naomi go in first. "Right?"

Once Naomi was walked by, I started quacking loudly and acting like a duck by tucking my thumbs into my armpits and flapping my elbows around like they were wings.

"*Quack, quack!*" I said super loudly, marching right

through door. "*Quack, quack, qua—*"

I stopped when I realized everyone was staring at me, and it was dead quiet, except for the few giggles here and there.

At the middle of the library stood a man with a mustache, a top hat, and a microphone. He was halfway up on the staircase, where there was an open section that turned and went the rest of the way up to the second floor. He looked like something from a steampunk comic book – the kind of old fashioned professor that built a time machine out of parts from a train.

The man's mustache was so large that it hid his lips when he spoke. It was only his mustache that quivered when his words came out. "Are you quite finished *quacking* now?" the man asked.

"Um…" I grunted since my brain was too busy packing its bags because it had given up on me. "Sorry," I finally managed to mutter.

A cricket chirped somewhere in the room. It was probably laughing at me too.

"Nerd," Naomi whispered with a smile as she walked past me.

The man with the mustache spoke awkwardly into the microphone, as if he didn't know to keep the mic a few inches from his face. "We'll wait until you're seated."

It was the longest walk I've ever had to make to try and find my friends. Every student in the library was watching as I filtered through the crowd of students. There was almost no noise, which meant that every time my book bag scraped across someone's clothing, it felt like it was screaming for everyone to gawk at me.

"Sorry ' bout that," I said when I bumped into a bunch of different kids. "Excuse me. Um, I'm sorry. *Sorrrrry!* Your book bag is blocking my—*thaaaanks*. Sorry!"

Finally, after what felt like a thousand hours, I found the rest of my friends sitting at one of the desks in the middle of the library. Zoe and Brayden had found the table, and were sitting next to each other.

On the other side of the table were Gidget and Slug. They were twins.

My ninja clan was only down to three members besides me. Gidget and Slug were two of them. Brayden was the third.

After months of trying to keep my ninja clan large, it was a relief to have such a small, loyal team. It was easier that way.

And then there was an empty seat with Faith sitting next to it.

Faith, for all those keeping track, had a secret of her own. I'd found myself in more than a few sticky situations at Buchanan, and Faith had been there to bail me out each time...but it *wasn't* as Faith. It was as the *white ninja*.

She knew I knew, but every time I brought it up, she changed the subject and acted like she didn't hear me. She was up to something. I just didn't know what yet. All I knew was that she was on my side, which was all that mattered.

Naomi was in front of me, pulling out the empty seat next to Faith.

Faith smiled at Naomi. "Sorry, this seat is for Chase."

My gut twisted because I knew my friends still didn't trust Naomi. "It's cool," I whispered. "She can have it. I'll just

27

stand… or sit on my knees next to you guys."

Faith exhaled slowly as Naomi took the seat next to her.

"Done yet?" the man with the mustache asked, but continued before I could answer. "Young man, another interruption from you, and I'll have to dole out a consequence."

I leaned toward Zoe. "Can he do that?"

Zoe's eyes grew wide as her eyebrows made a "V" shape on her forehead. "Chase, this guy can do whatever he wants, so *stop* talking! Put your lips together, and keep them that way!"

A low chuckle came from the speakers. The man with the mustache spoke. "It's alright, Zoe. Apparently your friend hasn't a clue as to who I am, so allow me to introduce myself… no, allow me to *re-introduce* myself since you were absent when I did it the first time."

Students in the library made an "*Ohhhhhhhh*," sound.

"My name," the man with the mustache said, pausing for effect, "is Dr. Ashley Tenderfoot."

"Oh, man," I whispered. I should've realized it was the guy Zoe was obsessing over.

The man had a big ol' mustache, a top hat, and a tuxedo

jacket, along with a pair of blue jeans and sneakers. And over his right eye was a tinted monocle.

I never understood the idea of a monocle. It was like someone said, *"I need glasses, but I'd like to use them for only half of the amount of eyes in my head."*

"I own and operate Tenderfoot Industries," Dr. Tenderfoot said. "Many of you are probably familiar with the work we've done, from hoverbikes to spaceship prototypes. And we're leading the way in state of the art robotics research. There's so much ground we've broken, but we've barely even scraped the surface!"

Zoe nudged me with her elbow. "See? This dude's awesome."

Tenderfoot continued as he stepped across the staircase platform. "Your president, Zoe Cooper, along with Principal Davis invited me to come and speak, which is something I *never* do, not because I don't like it, but because I'm much too busy to speak at every event I'm invited to. However," Tenderfoot paused. "There was something *different* about this time. I couldn't put my finger on it, but something told me I *had* to come and see the school for myself."

Tenderfoot paused again, tapping his finger on the railing of the staircase. He was looking right at me.

He blinked, turning his attention to the other students in the library. "Zoe and your principal really wanted to '*wow*' everyone, and show you that there's a whole world of undiscovered territory in the technological world."

Taking a step up on the stairs, Tenderfoot wrapped the cable of the microphone around his wrist.

"Some of the best tech that will exist a hundred years from now hasn't even been *thought* up yet," the mustached man said. "Think of the craziest science fiction movie you've ever seen..."

I heard a couple kids whisper names of movies to each other.

"Now imagine that to be the world you live in," Tenderfoot continued. "Massive spaceships orbiting the Earth, so large that all you see are their vague silhouettes in the clear blue sky. A weekend trip to see the rings of Saturn. An *actual* journey to the center of the Earth!"

"That *would* be sweet," Brayden whispered at me from across the table.

Tenderfoot's mustache raised on one side. I think he was smiling. "Keep this between us because it's a secret, but we've even got our best minds working on a little gadget that will allow *squids* to communicate with humans."

"No way," Slug said, not even trying to hide behind a quiet voice.

Tenderfoot chuckled. "Yes way!" he said. "Did you know squids are considered the most intelligent invertebrates in the world?" Tenderfoot closed his eyes, nodded, and held out a hand. "It's controversial, of course, but that doesn't stop our scientists from trying to have a conversation with them.... or even challenging them to a videogame or two. I can't say too much about it, but what I *will* say is this... squids are quite the talkers."

Brayden leaned into the table again. "Dude," he said quietly. "*Squid people!* Can you imagine? What if they got so smart they could go to school? Oh, man, what if we had classes with *squids?*"

"Cray craaaaay, I sang.

Zoe lightly slapped the table. "They'd still get better grades than both of you! Now pay attention!"

Tenderfoot was still talking into the microphone. "...which is the *real* reason I'm here this week. President Zoe, Principal Davis, and I have come up with a little competition for a handful of lucky students. Three teams will be chosen to build a fully functioning robot that—"

Someone from the back of the library shouted, interrupting Dr. Tenderfoot. "*Build* a robot? Are you kidding me? Half the kids here don't even know how to make a paper airplane!"

Everyone turned to see who had the guts to be so rude. It was a kid named Jake, and he was standing with a bunch of his friends, also known as "*the wolfpack.*"

Dr. Tenderfoot paused, smoothing his mustache out with his fingers. His patience was being tested. "If you'd let me finish, then you'd have heard me explain further that the robots don't have to do anything fancy. All it needs is one function, be it as simple as turning a switch to make it move from point A to point B. As long as it does *something*. Even the simplest, meaningless action counts. The goal is to *create*, and bring life to something that didn't have life before."

"Okay," Jake said annoyingly. "But that still sounds too

30

complicated for anyone in this room. I mean, c'mon, Buchanan students aren't the freshest eggs at the store."

Faith furrowed her eyebrows as she stared into space. "Freshest eggs at the store?" she repeated, confused.

Dr. Tenderfoot sighed. His fingers moved from smoothing his mustache, to pinching the spot between his eyes. "Parts for the project will be provided for by Tenderfoot Industries. It won't be *quite* as difficult as you're making it sound, but lucky for you, the odds of you being on a team are pretty slim."

Jake sunk back into the crowd.

"To keep everything simple," Dr. Tenderfoot continued, "there will only be three teams for the robotics competition that will be held on Friday morning. The winning team of the competition will receive a prize greater than they can even imagine."

The students in the library mumbled again to each other. This time there was excitement in the air. I heard a couple kids say something about how the prize was a million bucks, cash. That sounded a little crazy, but you know how people can get when they dream.

It's not like I was going to enter, but for some reason I was nervous that I'd somehow get roped into it, which gave me a queasy feeling in my stomach.

"I think it'd be totes sweet to compete," my cousin whispered. "But not just anyone can enter. Team leaders will be chosen out of Dr. Tenderfoot's hat."

And just like that, the queasy feeling was gone. "Nice," I said. "I never entered my name anywhere so I definitely *won't* get picked, which is good because I seriously need to recharge my batteries. Just *once*, I'd like to not be in the middle of an exciting adventure. I don't need to try and build a robot on top of all the other stuff on my mind."

"It's cool," Zoe said with a devious smile. "Because everyone's name was printed on slips of paper that I spent all night cutting out and folding in half. We're *all* entered whether we like it or not."

I groaned, letting my head fall to the table with a *thud*. I rolled my head back and forth, massaging my forehead with the hard wooden surface.

I rolled my head so far over that I could see the entrance to the library. And then something caught my eye from the skinny window on the door.

As Tenderfoot kept talking, I saw it again – a flash of red and green from the window.

"Holiday ninjas," I whispered.

"Holiday what?" Zoe asked.

"Um," I said, standing from my seat. "Nothing. Could you watch my stuff for a second?"

"Watch your stuff?" Zoe said quietly. "What do I do if someone tries to take it? Fight them? Hey, where are you going?"

Zoe was gonna be mad that I got up from the table, but she'd forgive me later. I knew there were red and green ninjas up to something in the halls, and I had to go check it out.

Principal Davis leaned against the wall next to the library doors. He didn't say anything when he saw me – just cocked an eyebrow.

I stopped, careful to speak quietly. "Uh, I gotta use the bathroom."

The principal sighed as he quietly pushed open the door.

Once I was out in the hallway, I waited until the library door clicked shut.

When I pulled my ninja mask over my face, I heard a boy's voice echo down the halls.

"Seriously?" the boy said. "I *made* you what you are!"

It was Wyatt… and it sounded like he was in trouble.

"Let's get dangerous," I whispered.

## Monday. 8:15 AM. The hallways.

Following Wyatt's voice led me out of the lobby. I found myself peeking around the corner of one the hallways down at the end of the school.

I was nervous because Wyatt wasn't even *trying* to keep quiet. It was almost like he *wanted* people to hear him. Too bad there weren't any teachers around. There were always teachers creeping around every corner when you didn't need them, but the first time you did, they weren't anywhere to be found.

About halfway down the hallway, I saw Wyatt pinned up against a water fountain that was between two bathrooms.

Two green ninjas stood in front of him doing their best ninja pose. It didn't look like they wanted to do anything except keeping Wyatt from getting away.

"I want your names!" Wyatt demanded. "When this is over, you're *so* getting kicked out of my ninja clan!"

"We're not even *in* your clan," one of the ninjas said.

"Just give us your mask," the other ninja said. "And we'll let you go. Easy peasy."

"There's no way I'm just gonna *give* you my mask," Wyatt growled.

So that's something I forgot to mention earlier. My last run in with the red and green ninjas happened because they were trying to swipe my ninja mask.

Wyatt had told me that the kid who got my mask would be the leader of the green ninjas. I only got away from them because I threw my mask down while they were chasing me. They were also after Wyatt's ninja mask for the same reason.

"Why do you need my mask anyways?" Wyatt said. "Word is that both the red and green ninja clans have their leaders. Whoever took my red ninjas from me made *himself* leader *without* my mask. And that noob, Chase, just let you *have* his mask!"

"Aw, thanks, Wyatt," I said quietly to myself. "It's not like I'm out here trying to help you."

I heard the ninja sigh. "Look, dude, you're washed up. You have no power over the red ninjas anymore, and our new orders are to take your mask anyway. We don't want you pretendin' to be a ninja."

"*Pretending?*" Wyatt said defensively. "Without *me*, the

35

red ninjas wouldn't even *exist!*"

"You wanna argue? Take it up with their new leader," the green ninja said. "I'm sure he'd *love* to have *that* conversation."

"I *would* if I knew who he was," Wyatt said.

"Their new leader?" the ninja asked. "That's easy, his name is—"

The other green ninja slapped his friend's shoulder. "Don't speak his name! That's the number one rule! And also the number two rule. Like, the first *ten* rules are that we never say his name!"

The two green ninjas took a step forward.

From where I was standing, I could see that Wyatt's hands were shaking. Not crazy shaking, but enough that was noticeable.

That kid had been such a pain to me since the first day of school. He's had it out for me since day one! And now there I was, trying to decide whether I should help him or not!

If this were a video game, I would've made both choices. I'd save the game right before helping him, and then see how it panned out after that. If it were the wrong choice, I'd just load my saved game so I could choose *not* to help him.

But this wasn't a game, and those ninjas *weren't* leaving Wyatt alone.

I clenched my jaw because I knew what I had to do. I never really had a choice because I decided a long time ago to try and do the right thing *every* time.

Stepping out into the middle of the hallway, I took a deep breath and shouted, "Hey, you guuuuuuuys!"

The two green ninjas turned to look at me.

"Leave him alone!" I said, trying to hide the fear in my voice. "You don't need anything else from him, so just let him walk!"

Wyatt shook his head at me. "I can handle this myself!"

I laughed. "Yeah, you're not pinned up against the water fountain or anything, right?"

The two ninjas in front of Wyatt stood up straight and relaxed the same way a bunch of football players do when the ref blows the whistle and the play was over. They looked like someone had called a timeout.

And then I knew why. I suddenly felt hands grab my arms. I tried to free myself, but there were too many people to shake myself free from. The ceiling felt like it was falling. The lights were only about a foot away from my face. I thought I was crazy in the brain until I realized...

They were picking me up.

Wiggling around to get free, I saw that Wyatt was also in the air. A bunch of ninjas were holding us over their heads.

"Give it back to me!" Wyatt growled.

One of the ninjas below was jumping up and down, victoriously waving Wyatt's red ninja mask in the air like it was a flag. I had managed to pull my own mask off before anyone got ahold of it.

"Let go of us!" I said, but obviously the ninjas didn't listen.

Instead, they ran through the halls carrying Wyatt and me over them. The fluorescent lights in front of my face zoomed by as the ninjas turned down different hallways.

The whole thing only lasted for ten seconds. The ninjas came to a stop right before the front lobby. I heard the sound of a door click, and then I realized what was about to happen.

The ninjas dumped Wyatt and me through the doors of

the library where all the students were still listening to Dr. Tenderfoot's presentation.

Our landing was so rough that both of us shouted in pain. Everyone in the library froze up, staring at the two nimrods making all the noise.

I was on my stomach. Next to me was Wyatt. His legs were on my back.

Zoe was glaring at me from the table she sat at. The rest of my friends looked shocked, like they were trying to make sense of what happened.

And Principal Davis was hovering above Wyatt and me with the angriest look I'd ever seen on his face.

Principal Davis helped me to my feet. "This is the second time *today* that you've caused a scene, Chase. And if Dr. Tenderfoot hadn't just announced your name, I'd send you right to my office."

"Announced my name?" I asked. "What're you talking

about?"

Wyatt dusted his pants off even though they didn't have dust on them.

Principal Davis put his hand on Wyatt's shoulder. "But since Dr. Tenderfoot didn't say *your* name, you need to head straight to the front offices and wait for me."

Wyatt didn't argue with the principal. He also didn't make eye contact. I thought maybe there were tears in his eyes, but he left the library before I could see.

Principal Davis put his hand on my shoulder and guided me through the crowd as they made a path for me to walk down.

"What're you doing?" I asked. "Where am I going?"

When I was standing in front of the staircase that Dr. Tenderfoot was speaking from, Principal Davis took his hand off me. Tenderfoot was holding his top hat in his hands. It was upside-down and filled with slips of paper.

Standing next to Tenderfoot were two other kids. One of them I knew well because it was Wyatt's cousin, Carlyle. The other was a student I only *kinda* knew. His name was Dante.

Carlyle had an ugly habit of talking like a pirate *all the time*. I know, right? *Super* annoying.

"Ah, the quacking child," Dr. Tenderfoot said as he studied me. "You must be Chase Cooper."

I tightened a smile because I didn't know what to say.

"Gratz to you, Chase Cooper," Tenderfoot said while waving a small slip of paper in front of him. "I've just chosen your name from my hat. You'll be the team leader of group C, or better yet, Team Cooper."

I sighed, feeling my stomach shrink in my belly. "Wonderful," I said.

### Monday. 8:30 AM. The library.

Since Dr. Tenderfoot was a special guest speaker, everyone's first period was cancelled. It gave kids a chance to speak with Dr. Tenderfoot about what Tenderfoot Industries was working on.

Stations were spread throughout the library. Different types of robots had been set up at each station. Flying drones. Tiny microbots smaller than the tip of a pencil. An android looking thing that freaked me out every time I looked at it.

I was still standing next to the staircase when my friends walked up.

Zoe was the first to say anything. "I can't believe you," she said. "You *knew* how important this morning was to me, and you were out in the hallways goofing off!"

"I wasn't!" I said. "I was out there because I saw—"

"I don't care if you saw Sasquatch out there," Zoe said. "You were playing around! You think the only person you affect with your little ninjas hijinks is yourself? It's not! Everyone who laughs at you is also laughing at me, Chase. You're embarrassing sometimes!"

Slug raised his eyebrows. "Dude, ouch," he said.

Zoe shut her eyes and shook her head. "I'm sorry," she

sighed. "I'm just feeling a little crazy because Dr. Tenderfoot is here. It wasn't easy to convince him to come, and I just wanted things to be perfect."

That whole morning was important to my cousin, and I interrupted it. *Twice.*

"No," I said. "I'm the one who's sorry. You're right. I should've stayed at the desk with you guys..."

"What's the deal with Wyatt anyway?" Naomi asked. "Why'd the two of you spill through the door?"

I thought about telling everyone about the red and green ninjas, but I didn't. I barely had any info about them so it wasn't the best time.

"It's nothing," I said. "I was just goofing off."

Zoe folded her arms and looked away. "You're lucky I'm the best cousin ever, or you'd be in the hot seat. Plus I *have* to forgive you since you're about to ask me to be on your team."

Scratching the back of my neck, I avoided eye contact with my cousin. "Um, I was actually going to find Dr. Tenderfoot and ask if I can pass on this."

"You're what?" Zoe asked, wide eyed.

"I'm spread too thin," I said honestly. Sitting on one of the steps on the staircase, I looked around the room, trying to find the man with the mustache.

Brayden's eyes opened huge, as if he was suddenly uncomfortable. "Uh, hey, guys, we should take a look at some of the Tenderfoot robots."

Our friends could tell that Zoe and I were about to argue. They wanted to bail so it wouldn't be awkward. Oh, how I wanted to bail with them.

I hoped Zoe would just drop it after everyone left, but she didn't.

"Chase," she said. "This is a *huge* opportunity for you. For us! Tenderfoot is someone who's going to be remembered for *centuries* because of his inventions! The fact that you've got a chance to sit down and talk with him one on one isn't something that comes along everyday!"

"I dunno," I said, still looking for Dr. Tenderfoot.

"Seriously, dude," my cousin said. "Like, in a hundred years, Buchanan School will probably be *filled* with the stuff he's created! People will be able to look back and say, 'okay, this is when the world changed because of Tenderfoot's inventions.'"

I listened to my cousin as I kept looking for Dr. Tenderfoot, but he wasn't anywhere I could see. His upside-down top hat was still sitting on the other end of the staircase. All the slips of paper with the names of students were stuffed inside it. The three slips of paper he had pulled out were folded neatly in half and resting next to the hat.

I leaned back, stretching my arm across the steps to grab the three slips of papers.

"I'm just so drained," I said to my cousin. "I'm like a tube of toothpaste that's totally empty, but keeps getting squished to get every last drop out."

"I still think you'd kick yourself later if you didn't at least *try* to work with Dr. Tenderfoot," Zoe said.

I kept quiet, but nodded my head as I played with the slips of paper from the top hat.

Zoe sat on the step next to me. "I know things are crazy for you right now," she said. "And I know that your ninja stuff is all out of whack."

I looked at Zoe. "You do?"

My cousin knew about my ninja clan, but I tried to keep most of that stuff a secret from her. I didn't want her stressing out over those things because it'd only make *me* stress out about them even more.

"C'mon," she said. "I'm not an idiot. Plus Faith and Gidget keep me in the loop."

"Awesome," I said sarcastically.

Zoe reached back and slid Dr. Tenderfoot's hat closer to us. "He's kind of a weird dude, isn't he? A fat mustache and a top hat with a tuxedo jacket, but with jeans and tennis shoes?"

"It doesn't surprise me. Most people like him are. Geniuses are an odd bunch."

"Oh, totes. Not in a bad way, but in a way that makes sense. Like, they think differently than everyone else, so they're naturally kinda… weird."

"I guess."

Zoe paused. "I wouldn't consider myself weird or anything like that. I became president because I worked hard. I set a goal. And then I took each step to get to the finish line."

"That's you though," I said. "Super organized and prepared for everything."

My cousin nodded. "But you're not like me," she said.

"You're impulsive and act without a plan. You do whatever you want and you don't care what anyone else thinks about you."

"Um, thanks?" I said.

"I think between the two of us, you're the most like Dr. Tenderfoot," Zoe said. "You're creative, weird, and totes cray cray, but you think differently than everyone else. Where someone sees a group of students, you see a ninja clan. I think you have it in you to win this robotics competition, but I really think you have it in you to become a great man like Dr. Tenderfoot."

Zoe was saying nice things, but I still wasn't sure if I wanted to be part of the competition.

And then my cousin's nose scrunched up as she tipped Dr. Tenderfoot's hat closer to her. Some of the slips of paper fell out.

She scooped them up and dropped them back into the hat. I grabbed a few slips too and shuffled them around on the step next to me.

Zoe looked away, waving to a friend across the room.

I dropped the rest of the paper back into Tenderfoot's top hat, but noticed something odd. Pushing one of the slips open with my fingers, I tried to find the name that was written on it... but it was blank. I did the same thing to several other slips. They were empty too.

All the slips of paper in Dr. Tenderfoot's hat were *blank*.

Zoe had said she was up half the night cutting and folding each piece of paper for the drawing. I doubt that she would've spent all that time on blank squares.

The slip of paper that should've had my name on it was empty too.

"What the heck?" I finally said a little too loudly.

"What's up?" Zoe said, looking back at me.

It was one of those moments that lasted an eternity. I almost spilled the beans about the blank slips of paper, but Tenderfoot was Zoe's hero. If I said anything about it, then she'd be heartbroken if he was gaming the system. But was it possible that he *wasn't* gaming the system, and there was a good explanation for what I had found?

Until I knew more, I thought it best to keep it from Zoe.

"Nothing," I said, pushing the slips of paper deeper into Tenderfoot's top hat. And then I scooted the whole thing just out of reach. "I mean, I should find Dr. Tenderfoot and tell him I'm out of the competition."

"Ugh," Zoe grunted as she rolled her eyes.

I thought she was grunting at me, but she wasn't. She grunted because of the kid who had strolled up to us.

"Ahoy, mateys," said a familiar voice with a gross pirate accent. "And where d'ya think yer goin' now?"

It was Carlyle, and he was standing at the bottom of the staircase, blocking our path.

Carlyle was the leader of his own little group of troubled students that called themselves pirates. They weren't *real* pirates, obvi, but that didn't stop them from dressing and talking like actual plunderers of the sea.

Back during my second month at Buchanan, Carlyle's pirate crew was huge. But lately, their club had lost most of its members. I'm pretty sure the only pirates left were Carlyle and a handful of other kids.

"Carlyle," I said to the pirate poser at the bottom of the staircase.

"Cooper," Carlyle replied, and then looked at Zoe. "Ahoy, lassie. Good t'see you, as always."

Even though I hated the way pirates talked, Zoe didn't. In fact, I was pretty sure she loved it.

"Hi," Zoe said.

"What do you want?" I asked.

"I'm here t'size up my competition," Carlyle said. "Ya best not try'n hornswaggle the game, mate, or ye'll find yerself in mess o'trouble ya can't clean."

I stared at the boy in front of me, totally confused. "*What* are you saying, dude?"

Carlyle smiled. He pointed his finger at me. "Ye might as well drop from the competition now, Chase! Don't even *bother* tryin' to build a robot 'cause it'll probably end up bein' super lame!"

I'm not sure what snapped inside me, but something did. I wasn't angry or anything like that. I felt the sudden drive to win at a game I didn't ask to play.

"Whatever, dude!" I said, stepping down the staircase to get right in the pirate poser's face. "You wanna know what? I was *going* to drop out of the competition, but now I *have* to compete just to wipe that smug pirate grin off your face!"

I heard Zoe squeal behind me, excited that I was going to play Tenderfoot's game.

Carlyle narrowed his eyes at me, but said nothing. He simply clicked his heels together, turned, and marched away.

**Monday. 2:45 PM. The science lab.**

At the end of the day, my friends and I met in one of the science labs on the second floor of the school. Zoe was there first, setting up the room so the three teams could have their own place to work.

I never found Dr. Tenderfoot to ask him about the blank slips of paper. I'd have to remind myself to ask him the next time he showed up. I wasn't too worried about it though. The fire in my belly was driving me to win – not to understand why a man would fill his top hat with blank paper.

Carlyle was in one corner of the room with the rest of his team – two kids dressed like pirates singing chanteys and swaying back and forth. It was as weird as it sounded.

It was also a much smaller team than I thought it'd be. The pirate threat at Buchanan School was definitely on the way out.

Dante was in another corner of the room, but he was all by himself. He must've *wanted* to be on his own team because Zoe said he never bothered asking anyone else.

My friends and I were all seated in our corner – Gidget, Slug, Brayden, Faith, Zoe, and Naomi. I knew it was a huge team, but there wasn't a limit on how many members I could have. I figured the more we had, the better our chances were at building a robot that *actually* worked.

The room was separated by three bed sheets hanging on lines like they were air-drying. Each team had their own corner of the science lab to work in. We could still hear everything going on in the room, but the teams couldn't see each other.

Naomi was in the middle of a conversation with Slug. "Y'see? You'll do it every time."

"Do what?" I asked, taking a seat.

Naomi looked at me with a blank expression. And then she made an ugly face.

I wasn't sure what was happening, so… I made an ugly face back at her.

Slug threw his arms up. "Dude, you just proved her right!"

"What?" I said, confused.

"Ugly faces are contagious," Naomi said smugly. "I can

make an ugly face at anyone in the school, and they'll throw one right back to me. Sometimes I just sit in the cafeteria making ugly faces. Every single time, someone else makes one when they see me, whether they know it or not."

HERS IS KINDA CUTE. MINE IS JUST... WOW.

"They're not contagious," I said. "I only did that because I knew what you were doing."

"Riiiight," Naomi said.

Gidget sat on one of the tall stools, staring at her cell phone. Without looking up, she said, "So *she's* really on our team?"

"You mean me?" Naomi asked.

Gidget never took her eyes away from the phone. "Bingo. No Scavengers allowed."

Naomi paused. "I'm not a Scavenger anymore," she said.

"What's a Scavenger?" Zoe asked.

"Nothing," I said. Zoe still didn't know who The

48

Scavengers were, and at that point, I didn't think it was important to tell her. The less she knew about them, the better off she was. "Yes, Naomi's gonna be part of the team. She's smart, and she's cool, and she's gonna help out a ton."

Gidget finally stopped thumb-jabbing her phone and glanced up with only her eyes. After a sigh, she finally said, "Whatever."

Gidget had the same problem with Naomi that Zoe did. It wasn't that they didn't like Naomi, but it was that they didn't want to see me get burned again.

Naomi put her hands on her hips and cleared her throat. "Can we move past this? I said sorry to Chase, and now I'm saying sorry to you guys. *Please*, can we just build this robot?"

Everyone on the team nodded, but like they didn't have a choice.

Team Cooper was off to a good start.

That was sarcastic... just sayin'.

If everyone was *this* unhappy about Naomi being on the team, I dreaded the moment I was going to tell them she was back in the ninja clan again.

Zoe took the lead. "So remember that we don't have to build a super awesome functioning robot – just a robot that can do *something*, like blink or just move forward."

"I think Tenderfoot just wants to see us create something that has some sort of function," Faith added.

"Seems a little hard for sixth graders, doesn't it?" Slug asked.

"That's exactly the kind of thinking a losing team would have," Gidget said. "Don't even get it in your brain that we *can't* do it. All we need to focus on is *how* we'll do it."

The fire in my belly grew stronger as I listened to my friends talk about how we weren't going to give up. It was one of the rare times we were able to work together as a group, and I knew that as long as we kept our heads up, almost nothing could stop us.

Nothing... except for maybe the red and green ninja clans.

**Tuesday. 7:15 AM. The science lab before school.**

    I got to school early the next morning. I used to struggle with waking up before school even *started*, but I was getting better at it.
    Plus I wanted to get there before the rest of my team. As the leader of the group, it was best for me to be the first one there every time.
    Tenderfoot Industries provided the parts to the robot we were going to build. Enough pieces were given to each team that all three robots wouldn't be exactly the same as each other.
    After we studied the pieces, my team chose what kind of robot we wanted to make. It wasn't anything crazy, but we still wanted to try and impress Dr. Tenderfoot with it.
    Most of my night was spent drawing blueprints and sketches of what I thought the robot should look like. With my background as a professional comic book reader, I thought I had come up with a sweet design.
    The blueprints and sketches were rolled up into tubes that I stuck between my book bag and my back, making it look like I was carrying ninja swords.
    The school was quiet when I walked into the lobby.

Principal Davis was standing inside the entrance wearing his Tuesday suit. His hands were in his pockets, and he was just staring at the parking lot outside.

When he noticed me, he snapped out of his trance. "Cooper," he said with a nod.

"Hey, Mr. Davis," I said.

"Better get upstairs," he said. "The rest of your team's already up there waiting for you."

"They are?" I said, surprised. So much for being the first one in the room.

I shuffled past the principal and headed for the elevator next to the cafeteria entrance.

The elevator doors opened the instant I pushed the button. I stepped through the doors, and then pushed the button for the second floor.

"Oh, and Chase?" Principal Davis said from the lobby.

The doors to the elevator hadn't shut yet. "Hmm?" I said, lifting my chin.

"I'm impressed with your choice in teammates," he said. "It takes a real man to forgive someone like that."

Principal Davis must've been talking about Naomi, but I wasn't sure how he knew anything about the history we had with each other. Oh well. I didn't want to read too much into it.

"Thanks," I said with a smile as the elevator doors shut.

It took another few minutes to get to the science lab on the second floor. My stomach was fluttering with butterflies, but it always did that whenever I used the elevator.

Finally, I pushed open the door to the science lab. Inside the room was a flurry of activity and excitement.

I couldn't see Carlyle's team because of the hanging bed sheets, but I could hear them "*Yaaaaring*" away as they banged metal against metal. If I didn't know it was them, I would've thought for sure that it was a buncha monkeys back there.

Dante's corner of the room was pretty quiet, but I could see the top of his head over the sheet. He was pacing back and forth, probably trying to brainstorm.

And then there was my team, Team Cooper, sitting on chairs they had formed a circle with. Principal Davis was right – everyone *was* already there.

Zoe, Faith, Brayden, Gidget, Slug, and Naomi sat in a circle talking to each other about how we were going to build the robot for the competition.

Someone must've brought pancakes for the group because they each had a plate with a short stack on their laps.

"Mmmm," I said, taking the seat next to Naomi. "Gimme some pancakes! Who brought 'em?"

"I did," said a voice from behind me.

My stomach scrunched into a tiny ball when I heard the voice because I knew who it was before I even turned around.

It was Wyatt, and he was holding a plate of pancakes meant for me. On top of his head was an oversized chef's hat. You know the kind – like a big mushroom looking thing. It was weird, but I *wasn't* surprised that he was wearing it.

"Eat up," Wyatt said.

I took the pancakes from him because I didn't know what else to do. If I hadn't, he'd just stare at me, waiting for me to take the breakfast he made.

A smile tightened on my face as I set the plate on my

lap. "Thaaaaaanks," I whispered.

"No prob, Bob," Wyatt said, wiping his hands on the apron he was wearing. "Oh! I almost forgot! I got whipped cream and syrup too. I'll go get them."

And then the principal's comment made sense. "*I'm impressed with your choice in teammates,*" and then something about forgiveness. Principal Davis thought Wyatt was on my team.

Wyatt walked back to the counter that was several feet away. It looked like he hijacked that spot and turned it into his own kitchen. There were cartons of buttermilk, bowls of pancake batter, cracked eggs, butter, whipped cream, syrup, and an electric griddle. Almost everything was covered in a thin layer of flour.

I leaned into the center of my circle of friends, careful not to let my pancakes fall off my lap. "What the heck, Zoe?" I whispered. "Why's he here?"

Zoe covered her lips with her hand and spoke through a mouthful of food. "Dude, his cakes are *amazing*. Like, seriously, it's like cooked happiness!"

"For real," Faith said.

Everyone else on the team nodded and mumbled the same kinds of things.

"No," I said, cutting my pancakes with a fork. Wyatt hadn't returned yet with the whipped cream and syrup, but I liked my pancakes plain anyway. "I mean, why's he even in here?" I asked, shoving a forkful of pancake in my mouth.

I gotta be honest. Wyatt whipped up a batch of killer pancakes.

I refused to admit it aloud, but my body spoke for me when I tilted my head back and sunk in my seat.

"See?" Zoe whispered. "I *told* you they were awesome!"

"Fine," I said. "They're good, but you haven't answered my question yet!"

Zoe sat up straight to make sure Wyatt was still out of earshot. "Um, we let him hang out because of *pancakes*, but we also didn't make him leave because *you're* the team leader, so it's *your* job to get rid of him!"

Faith shrugged. "You're the boss," she added.

I groaned, but took another bite of pancake. I wasn't as polite as Zoe. I spoke all loud with a mouthful of food. "Whatever, I'll ask him to leave when he gets back with—"

"Ask who to leave?" Wyatt said, standing next to me with a can of whipped cream and a bottle of syrup.

"Ummmm," I said, shoveling another bite of pancake into my mouth. I asked him to leave, but with all the food in my cheeks, it just sounded like muffled gibberish.

Wyatt's body slumped as he lowered the whipped cream and syrup. "You're talking about me, aren't you?" he said quietly. "You wanna ask me to leave?"

Nobody in the group answered. Instead, they stared at me, waiting for *my* answer.

But before I could say anything, Wyatt spoke. "C'mon, dude, *please* let me be on your team. I'll do anything to help. Whatever you need! I'll be the coffee guy! Or the pancake guy! I know we've butted heads before, but I'm tellin' ya that I *want* to change! It's just that… I don't… I don't really have any friends anymore."

The others on the team didn't know Wyatt lost his ninja clan, but I did. I knew better than my friends what Wyatt was feeling, and I couldn't help but feel sorry for him.

Wyatt grew impatient and pointed at Naomi. "I mean, c'mon! You let *her* on the team! She burned you to your core! All I did was… well, nevermind what *I* did. If Naomi's on the team, then why can't I be?"

Naomi said nothing. She was embarrassed that Wyatt called her out.

"Bro!" Wyatt said. "You gotta be like water!"

I looked Wyatt dead in the eye. "What'd you say?"

"Be like water," he repeated.

A chill ran down my spine. Real Wyatt had said the same thing as Dream Wyatt.

But… aside from the strange déjà vu, Wyatt *wasn't* wrong. Naomi *was* on the team, but we were good friends again. I forgave her, even if the rest of my team was a little behind on it.

I couldn't shun Wyatt after welcoming Naomi back with open arms, could I?

Shutting my eyes, I took the last bite of my pancakes. "Fine," I whispered.

"I'm sorry," Gidget said, leaning closer to me. "What was that?"

"Open your earballs, ya old lady," Wyatt said to Gidget.

Gidget rested her cell phone on her lap and spoke calmly

while she looked at Wyatt. "I have a soul crushing comeback for that, but I'm gonna stop myself from saying it 'cause it'll *wreck* you *so bad* that your *children* will feel the burn. They'll *cry* themselves to sleep, but they *won't* know why. And when you see their tears... you'll remember *me*."

Wyatt's voice turned to a whisper. "Geez..."

"She's tellin' the truth, man" Slug warned Wyatt.

My eyes were still shut. "Wyatt can be on the team too," I forced myself to say.

The rest of the team started talking at the same time, shocked at my decision. It was too much for me to understand what anyone was saying except that they were all pretty unhappy about it.

Wyatt tightened one side of his mouth. "Guys, it's cool," he said sadly. "I get it. I know when I'm not wanted... I'll just... get some breakfast or something... by myself."

As he walked out, I could tell he was hurt.

And the war that was going on in my head was driving me crazy!

Wyatt has been the bad guy since the first day of school! He's been against me at every twist and turn! He's done *so many* bad things that I should've been *happy* about him walking away, but I wasn't!

Everyone deserved second chances, didn't they? Or *third*, or *fourth* chances, I guess?

What if *that* was the point in Wyatt's life that defined if he was a good guy or a bad guy? If I let him leave broken, he'd be hurt and probably carry a heavier grudge against me... but if I let him on the team, then maybe, just maybe, he'd stop being such a jerk!

Wyatt was at the counter, putting all the pancake ingredients into a plastic grocery bag.

My friends returned their attention to the project for the competition.

I was still chewing on my last bite of pancakes because I didn't want to swallow it since my stomach was all twisted up over Wyatt.

Finally, I swallowed my bite and sighed heavily because I knew what I had to do. It might not have been what I *wanted* to do, but sometimes you gotta get outta your bubble and do the right thing.

Wyatt was at the door.

"Wait!" I said.

Stopping in place, Wyatt glanced over his shoulder. The way he did it was creepy, and not helpful in making him seem like less of a villain, but I ignored it since that's kinda who he was.

"You can be on the team," I said. "But you can't sit around. You gotta actually help us build this robot, alright?"

Wyatt turned, his body straightening out as he did. He marched back to our circle a little *too* victoriously.

And his voice was bright and loud. "Thanks, bro," he said, setting his grocery bag of ingredients down on the floor. He pulled a seat up to the group, flipped it backwards, and sat on it, resting his arms on the back of the chair. "So… when do we start?"

As if to answer Wyatt's question, the door to the science lab opened. One of the lunch staff was peeking her head in, and then pointed at Wyatt. "You!" she said accusingly. "You left the kitchen before you paid for *any* of those ingredients! I said you could take what you wanted as long as you *bought* them!"

Wyatt leaned back, stretching his arms way out like he had just woken up. "Oh," he said with a smirk. "Chase'll be paying for all of it. The pancakes were for my… I mean, *his* team."

The woman on the lunch staff looked at me, waiting for an answer.

I sighed. "Sure," I said, digging my wallet out of my book bag. "I got it."

Wyatt wasn't exactly *lying*.

The pancakes *were* for the team.

…right?

### Tuesday. 11:30 AM. Lunch.

The rest of the team wasn't happy with my decision to let Wyatt on the team, but they didn't fuss anymore about it. They knew I was making the right decision even if it wasn't the one they would've made.

It helped that I vouched for Wyatt too. I told them that it was my own mistake to make, but I felt like he really wanted to start a new chapter in his life. I just hoped I wasn't wrong.

Zoe even came up to me afterward and apologized, telling me that giving Wyatt a shot on the team was the "grown-up" thing to do. Then she slugged me in the arm, like, *way* too hard, the way she always does.

Faith would probably slug my arm in the same spot later in the day. Those two seemed to always punch me in the same spot on the same day, and repeatedly… like they had planned it…

Aaaand I'm just realizing now that they probably *do* plan it like that. I'm such a noob sometimes.

Once I got my food from the kitchen, I stepped into the cafeteria to find a seat. Lunch was a *hamburger*. Not a *cheeseburger*. A *hamburger*.

I know, right? Why would anyone make a cheeseburger

with no cheese?

Oh well, I was still stuffed from the pancakes that Wyatt made before school, so I opted for the Buchanan School student favorite - French fries with mayonnaise and ketchup, along with a bowl of broccoli cheese soup. Blanketing the soup with pepper was optional, but I always did it.

Team Cooper was sitting at a table across the room, waving at me to join them, so I started walking in their direction.

About halfway across the cafeteria, I heard Wyatt call out my name. He was sitting on the stage with his legs crossed. His girlfriend, Olivia Jones, was sitting next to him, taking a bite from a cheese-deprived cheeseburger.

I nodded at him, but continued toward my friends.

"Wait," Wyatt said. "I have some things to talk to you about."

Stopping in place, I looked back at where my friends were seated. There was still plenty of time left for lunch, so I guess I had a few minutes to stop and hear what Wyatt had to say.

Resting my tray on the stage, I hopped up, and slid closer to Wyatt and Olivia, which was a completely new feeling for me to *choose* to sit near Wyatt.

I had to get outta my bubble, right?

Olivia smiled her awkward smile. She had gotten braces since the last time I talked to her. "Hi, Chase."

I smiled back.

"This isn't easy for me," Wyatt said as Olivia put her hand on his as if to comfort him. "But I wanted to thank you for letting me join your team."

"Yeah," Olivia said. "It was pretty cool of you."

"Well, I'm a pretty cool guy," I joked.

"Did you hear that the mystery prize is a million dollars?" Olivia said.

"No way," I said. "There's no way! A million dollar prize for a lame-o sixth grade robot project? Between only three teams?"

"Tenderfoot's a billionaire," Wyatt said. "A million bucks to him is nothing. I'm buyin' a *boat* when I win. I mean, when *we* win."

I had my doubts about the rumor, but it *was* a little exciting to think about.

Anyway, if you've followed my life at all, you'd know how weird it was that Wyatt and Olivia were being nice to me, or even talking to me at all.

THIS IS **OLIVIA** THIS IS WHAT HAPPENS WHEN SHE FAKES A SMILE...

Since they were being so kind, I took a chance and asked a hard question. "What's up with those ninjas yesterday? Why'd they corner you and throw us into the library?"

Wyatt's face tensed, but he quickly relaxed. "I'm only talking to you about it because you let me on your team," he said.

"Cool."

"You remember that the red and green ninja clans were trying to steal our masks, right?" Wyatt said quietly.

Olivia's face looked sad.

"Right," I said. "Whoever got our masks would be the leaders of those ninja clans."

"That's really all there was too it," Wyatt said. "The green ninjas have their new leader because they got your mask

59

last week. The red ninjas have their leader already, but they still wanted to send me a message by taking mine."

"What was the message?" I asked.

"Get lost," Olivia said, answering for her boyfriend.

"Do you know who the leaders are?" I said.

"No." Wyatt shook his head. "No clue. I showed up one day to training and was booted right out of my own ninja clan."

"Did you do something that made them mad?" I said.

Wyatt took a deep breath. "My red ninja clan had gotten too big for me to control by myself. The rest of my ninjas knew it too. They questioned my leadership skills and wanted to do things I *didn't* want to do."

"Like what?" I said, dipping some fries in my broccoli cheese soup, and then shoving them into my mouth. Hey, don't knock it 'till ya try it.

"Dumb things," Olivia said. "Like they wanted to start a website and sell t-shirts and other junk!"

"We're a ninja clan!" Wyatt said. "Not a business!"

I continued chewing on my awesome broccoli cheese fries, nodding and listening as Wyatt went on.

"So I guess everyone thought they could do a better job of being a leader," Wyatt continued. "And that's exactly what happened – one day, everyone stopped listening to me, and started doing whatever they wanted. It wasn't even like there was anyone loyal to me at all after that. Nobody sided with me. And that's when I lost complete control."

"But what about the kid who ordered everyone to steal our masks?" I said.

"Nobody was listening to *me*," Wyatt said, "but when *someone else* stood up and spoke, they were all ears. The group was falling apart because it had nobody to lead it, and they knew it. They just needed a little direction from someone who *wasn't* me."

"And that's when they gave the order to take our masks," I added.

"Not quite," Wyatt said. "I *thought* that stealing my mask would choose a leader for the red ninjas, but I was wrong about that. They already had their leader. They just wanted to boot me from the game."

Olivia continued explaining. "And then someone decided that stealing *your* mask would be just as awesome," she said to me, "which is when the idea for the green ninja clan was born."

I shrugged my shoulders. "No big deal. I got a million ninja masks in my locker."

"The red and green ninja clans are basically sister clans," Wyatt said. "They're working together, but wearing different colors."

"Holiday ninjas," I whispered, taking another bite of fries.

Olivia snickered at my joke.

Wyatt paused, and then spoke again after another deep breath. "Which brings us to the reason why I wanted to be on your robot team."

"Of course," I said, feeling embarrassed that I might've fallen for another one of Wyatt's tricks.

"No!" he said defensively. "It's not like that. I honestly wanted to get on your good side, because… well, I need your help."

I shook my head, disappointed. "Go on…"

"I want to work *with* you to figure out what to do about the red and green ninjas," he said. "Letting them continue is just crazysauce, right? I mean, those kids are *dangerous!*"

"So what do you wanna do?" I asked, not sure if I wanted to hear the answer.

Wyatt smiled, but it was genuine. "I just want things to go back to normal, like the good ol' days, with only the red ninjas versus the black ninjas."

I LOL'd. "Normal?" I said. "Normal for you is to have only *one* enemy? Normal for me is to have *no* enemies!"

"I'm not saying we should be enemies!" Wyatt said. "I'm saying that maybe we should team up and be… *frenemies*. C'mon, think about it. You wanna deal with *two* ninja clans who are out to get you?"

I swallowed my fries hard. I hated that Wyatt was *kind of* making sense. I had no idea who the leaders of the new ninja clans were. With Wyatt, I at least *knew* who *he* was.

But Wyatt's plan was to make it so it was only his ninja clan against mine. I needed more than that if I was gonna help him.

Finally, I said, "I'll help you under one condition."

"Name it," Wyatt said seriously.

"Once we figure this thing out with those other two ninja clans, we stop being against each other," I said. "No more enemies. We don't have to be friends, but we're definitely not enemies."

"You're telling me to give up my ninja clan?" Wyatt asked, narrowing his eyes.

"No," I said. "Two ninja clans can exist in the school without ever bumping into each other. You leave mine alone. That's all I want."

Wyatt didn't hesitate. "Deal," he said.

Olivia swooned over her boyfriend. "I'm so proud of you, babe!"

Wyatt leaned back, smiling smugly.

And for the first time in a long time, I saw a shimmer of hope for the future. A truce with Wyatt would be an epic win for me. Of course, there was always the chance it would turn into an epic fail. Wyatt could easily backpedal on the truce.

All I could do was hope for the best.

**Tuesday. 2:46 PM. The science lab.**

Naomi met me in the lobby, next to the statue of James Buchanan, and together we headed up the stairs to the science lab on the second floor.

"Yo," Naomi said.

"Whaddup?" I replied.

"Nothing. I just wanted to walk into the science lab *with* you."

I paused. "Because you feel like everyone hates you?"

Naomi didn't answer, which meant I was right.

"They don't," I said. "They might not be happy with you right now, but they'd never *hate* you."

"They might. Kids can change their minds about people."

"Right," I said. "But I think it's one of those things where you gotta give it a little time. It'll be weird at first, but once they see that you're the real deal, they'll warm back up to you."

Naomi smiled. "You really think it's that easy?"

I nodded, smiling.

"I don't even know why I'm spazzing over this," Naomi said, lightly laughing. "I thought I didn't care about what others think about me."

I belted out a laugh. "I don't care who you are, or what age you are. I'm pretty sure I'll always care about what people think of me. I can ignore it, but that doesn't mean I don't care."

"As long as you got someone to talk to?" Naomi said, finishing my thought.

Again, I nodded with a smile.

"At least with Wyatt on the team," Naomi said, "everyone has something *else* to focus on besides me. It's cool that you let him on Team Cooper. I couldn't do it. I'd be too paranoid about him."

"Well, I'm not gonna lie," I said. "I got a terrible feeling in my butt about it."

"What? Your butt?" Naomi asked, super confused.

"Yeah," I said. "Y'know, a butt feeling. I got a terrible butt feeling about it."

Naomi laughed, but she caught it in her throat and coughed. "*Gut* feeling! You got a terrible *gut* feeling about it!"

"Ohhhh," I said, embarrassed. But not just embarrassed because of that one moment. I was suddenly feeling the embarrassment from a *lifetime* of saying it wrong. "I'm an idiot."

Naomi tried to hide her smile, but she couldn't.

Another minute later, and we were standing outside the science lab. Pushing open the door, I let Naomi go in first, because y'know… ladies first.

From the moment I entered the room, all I could hear were the sounds of hammers and drills.

My team was to the right, hunched over the blueprints I drew up the night before. Wyatt was in the middle of the group.

I couldn't see the Carlyle or Dante's sections of the room. The sheets that Zoe had put in place worked well. It would've been easy for any team to sneak a look at their competition by peeking over one of the sheets, but the fact that Zoe was in the room made them nervous to cheat like that. I mean, she *was* the president of the school, which demanded at least a *little* respect.

Even though I couldn't see the other teams, I knew that Carlyle's team didn't have more than the few kids I saw before. I only heard the voices of two or three students from his side of the room.

Dante's side was super quiet. Like, dead quiet. If I didn't see his shadow moving on the sheet, I would've sworn there was nobody over there.

"Is Dante still on his own?" I asked Naomi.

She nodded. "I think so. Zoe said something about Dante being the quiet loner type. Not creepy loner, but just… quiet."

"She said the same thing to me too," I said. "That Dante never even tried to get anyone else on his team."

"Oh, that's not true," Naomi said. "I heard he asked some peeps, but they said no."

I sighed. "Bummer."

Naomi and I grabbed a couple empty chairs and joined the rest of our team.

Zoe chewed on the end of a pencil as she held my blueprints in front of her. Faith was next to her pointing at different spots of my drawings and quietly commenting on them.

Gidget was busy tapping away on her cell phone. It looked like she wasn't interested in the project, but I knew that whatever she was doing on her phone had everything to do with the project. That's just how she was.

Slug… was slouched over with his hands on his round belly. He looked like he had just finished off his tenth plate at a pizza buffet.

Brayden was next to him, munching away on some kind of tortilla thing filled with cheese and meat. It was too thin to be a taco, which meant it was probably…

"Quesadillas," Slug slurred with his eyes half open, but he pronounced it *kay-suh-dill-ahs*. "Wyatt made chicken quesadillas for the group. I might've had one too many…"

"How many did you eat?" I asked.

"Eight," Slug answered, breathing heavily.

"Eight quesadilla triangles?" I said, grossed out.

Slug shook his head. "No… eight *full* quesadillas," he said, again pronouncing it wrong.

"Dude," I said, my jaw dropping to the floor. "That's, like, um… four times eight… *thirty four slices!*"

Naomi quickly corrected me. "Thirty *two* slices."

"Thirty *two* slices!" I repeated.

"This kid can pack 'em away!" Wyatt said, bringing

another plate of quesadillas to the group.

"Gidgy…" Slug said, reaching for his twin sister, who was scooting away from his greasy fingers. "I might need a stomach transplant after this."

"Gross," she said. "Don't touch me. And stomach transplants aren't a real thing."

FAITH.
DISTRACTED
BY FOOD.

WYATT.
LOOKIN' ALL
CREEPER.

GIDGET.
GROSSED
OUT.

SLUG.
FAT &
HAPPY.

KICK
THE
COOK

"Giiiiidgy!" Slug groaned. "We're *twins!* Your stomach is an exact match for mine! Only *you* can save me! I only need *half* of it. The other half'll grow back!"

"Dude," Gidget said, raising an eyebrow. "You can't have my stomach."

"But what if I *need* it?" Slug whined, sliding lower in his chair. "You're just gonna—"

And then Slug let out the grossest burp I'd ever heard in my life. It was loud, and it was bad. Like, my eyes started watering.

Slug instantly sat up in his seat with a smile beaming across his face. "All better," he said, reaching for another quesadilla on Wyatt's plate. "Mmmm, gimme, gimme,

gimme!"

Gidget looked disgusted as she shook her head ever so slightly at her twin brother. "Hashtag, *so* gross."

Slug stuffed the loaded tortilla into his mouth and chomped loudly, leaning closer to his sister to annoy her. "Did you hear my face fart?"

"Get away!" Gidget said.

Gidget might've had an attitude about it, but she was obviously having fun. That was the kind of relationship she had with her brother because she laughed loudly as she pushed her elbow into Slug to keep him away.

"Stop it!" she squealed.

It reminded me a lot of how Zoe and I were with each other.

"Wyatt makes the best quesadillas," Faith said. "We've appointed him as the official chef for Team Cooper."

Wyatt nodded and faked the kind of laugh a politician would have. "Hey, I'll take what I can get," he said, presenting a quesadilla to Faith.

"I thank ye, kind sir," Faith said as she took a tortilla off the plate.

"My pleasure, m'lady," Wyatt replied, nodding.

Even Zoe chuckled, shaking her head at Wyatt as she took a quesadilla triangle from him.

I thought it was gross.

It was shocking how quickly my team had warmed up to Wyatt. Not that I cared … I just thought it was gonna take a little more time.

And then I noticed Olivia sitting way off to the side. I missed her the first time because she wasn't with the group. Instead, she was on a seat that was backed against the wall. And she did *not* look happy.

"Why's she over there?" I asked, pointing to Wyatt's girlfriend. "And why's she wearing her pouty face?"

Brayden sat up, pushing his chest out, and beating on it twice like a caveman. "She's allergic to my cologne," he said proudly. "She has a sneezing fit whenever she gets close."

"Ironic, isn't it?" Zoe said. "The thing you're spraying yourself with is to *attract* girls, but instead, you're *repelling* them."

"I know, right?" Brayden said, rolling his eyes. "But I've allowed myself time to learn how to use the cologne

67

properly."

"Allowed yourself time?" Zoe repeated, lowering the blueprints to get a better look at Brayden. "Allowing yourself time until what? Until you woo all the ladies in the world with your musk?"

Brayden snapped two fingers and pointed at my cousin. "Totes correct," he said slyly.

Zoe did her best to hide her smile. "Oh, geez."

I looked at Olivia again, who was still pouting against the wall.

OLIVIA'S POUTY FACE 😠!!!

"I don't care that she's here," I said, "but does she have to be? If her nose holes are makin' her sneeze, then why would she stick around?"

"She's here for me," Wyatt said, waving at his girlfriend, who didn't wave back. "Her presence comforts me."

"That's such a weird way to say that," I said. But after I looked at Faith, she smiled at me, and I knew exactly what Wyatt was talking about.

"I vouch for her," Wyatt said. "Just like how you vouched for me. How's that?"

"Okay," I said, not really caring. "She can stay. As long as she doesn't mess up our flow."

Wyatt nodded seriously. "Of course," he said. "She's cool over there."

The door to the science lab swung open, and one of Dr. Tenderfoot's employees wheeled in a flat panel television.

"Students," the employee said. "Students, if you could take a moment to look up here, Dr. Tenderfoot has recorded a message for you."

Everyone in the room stopped what they were doing and stepped out from behind their sheets. Carlyle was with his pirate buddies. Dante was on his own, covered in grease from working on his robot.

The employee waited a moment for everyone to quiet down, and then he took a small cassette from his shirt pocket and inserted it into a slot on the back of the television.

The screen flipped on and showed Dr. Ashley Tenderfoot's face, complete with old-fashioned mustache, top hat, and monocle over his right eye.

"Hello," Tenderfoot said. "First of all, I'd like to congratulate *all* of you for being selected for the competition. I'm sure that Carlyle, Dante, and Chase have chosen their teams wisely, so be proud if you're listening to this message."

Some kids looked at Dante because he didn't have a team standing behind him. Tenderfoot's message about choosing team members wisely didn't apply to him, and he was obviously embarrassed.

With all the excitement in the past twenty-four hours, I had completely forgotten about being randomly selected from Tenderfoot's top hat. The slips of paper from his hat were blank. If you asked me, that weighed pretty heavily on the mystery scale.

My brain was so busy running that I missed the rest of Tenderfoot's video message. All I caught was the very last part.

"...and I thank you again for playing your part in this historic competition," he said. After that, Tenderfoot tipped his top hat down, and the video stopped.

The employee from Tenderfoot Industries removed the cassette and pushed it into his front pocket. Wheeling the television out the door, he looked over his shoulder, said "G'day," and left the room.

The other teams moved back behind their bed sheets and continued their work.

Faith said what everyone else was thinking. "Tenderfoot's weird."

"Who records a video message like that?" Wyatt said.

"Dr. Tenderfoot is a super busy man," my cousin said defensively. "I'm just happy that he sent us *any* kind of message."

I pondered for a moment... that's such an "adult" sounding thing to say, isn't it? Pretend I have an old school gentleman's voice. "Mmmmm, yes, I *pondered* for a moment..."

The cassette had me thinking. I turned to Zoe and spoke. "Remember when I was talking about hiding messages to our future relatives in the school? Like, a hundred years from now, I could talk to my great grandkids or whatever?"

Zoe sighed, shutting her eyes. "Yeaaaaaaaaah," she said.

"I could record videos like Tenderfoot did!" I said, excited. "I could hide them all over the school and send our great grandchildren on treasure hunts and stuff!"

Slug nodded, scratching his chin. "I like the way you think, mister."

"No way," Wyatt said abruptly. "In a hundred years,

cassette tapes won't even exist. I'm surprised Tenderfoot even used one! Think about it – do you send messages using Morse code?"

Gidget was the one who answered, still jabbing at her cell phone with her thumbs. "Um, no way, dude."

"Exactly," Wyatt said. "Let's say you *did* leave a bunch of cassettes hidden in the school, and your great great great grandkids found them."

"Okay?" I said.

"They probably wouldn't even know what to do with them!" Wyatt said, and then he pretended to inspect an invisible cassette in his hand. "They'd be like, 'what the heck is this thing?'"

"I'm sure cassette tapes will still be used," Brayden said.

"You know what the very first records looked like?" Wyatt asked.

Slug perked up. "What's a record?"

Wyatt pointed at Slug. "Exactly," he said. "One, most kids don't even know what a record is, and two, the very first records looked like tubes. Not the flat discs people are familiar with."

"But people can still play records," Naomi said.

"Give it another fifty years," Wyatt said. "And records won't even exist at all anymore, except maybe to hardcore antique collectors."

Slug raised his hand. "Wait, I'm still not entirely sure what a *record* is still. You can play it? Like, in a game or something?"

Gidget lowered her head, rubbing the bridge of her nose. "Dude…"

"In a hundred years, I bet there will be something *way* cooler than cassettes," Wyatt said. "They'll probably be beaming information right onto their eyeballs."

Arguing about cassette tapes with Wyatt was something I didn't care to do, so I nodded.

Although, learning stuff by having the information beamed right into my eyeballs *did* sound pretty awesome… maybe Tenderfoot Industries was already working on that.

Oh man, how *cool* would that be?

**Tuesday. 3:00 PM. The science lab.**

After our cassette tape conversation, my team separated into four groups.

Zoe and Faith dealt with the moving parts of our robot.

Slug and Brayden worked on the shell of the robot because, c'mon, ya can't make a robot without it looking awesome.

Gidget and Naomi were buddied up to figure out what parts we still needed.

And finally, I paired myself with Wyatt. I knew if anyone else had to work with Wyatt, they wouldn't be happy about it. Plus it meant I could keep on eye on him in case there *was* something fishy about him being there.

We were in charge of problem solving things like trying to make the robot work better with less parts and stuff.

Our group was spread out in our section of the science lab. We were close enough to hear one another, but far enough that our conversations could still be private.

Dante's voice exploded from behind his partition. "Stupid machine! Just *work* already! I'm doing everything right, why won't you just work?"

"Whoa," Slug said. "Someone's having problems."

Dante's shadow moved back and forth on the white sheet. And then he raised his foot and kicked at another large shadow, knocking it over. The sound of small screws and metal parts bouncing off the floor filled the air.

"Way to go, Dante," he said to himself. "Messed things up again, didn't you? It's not the robot's fault it doesn't work, it's *yours*."

We all watched as Dante's shadow stood perfectly still. After a moment, he walked out from behind the sheet and left the room.

"Yikes," Brayden said.

The rest of my team looked at each other, but got back to work after a few seconds. We all agreed that Dante probably had to blow off some steam and start fresh the next day.

Wyatt slid a chair next to mine and flipped it around again, sitting on it backwards with his arms on the backrest. Quietly, he asked, "So what do you think we should do about the red and green ninja clans?"

"Hmm?" I hummed. "Oh, I don't know. I haven't thought about it yet."

"Time's runnin' out, Chase," Wyatt said. "The longer it

takes us to make a move, the larger those two ninja clans get."

"Make a move?" I said. "What kind of move are you talking about?"

"I got a couple ideas."

I glanced over my shoulder. The rest of my team was behind me, working on their section of the robot, and there I was, talking ninja clan stuff with my... *frenemy*.

"What're your ideas?" I asked.

"Well," Wyatt said, sitting up straight. "I have three ideas. The first one, is that we find the leaders of the two ninja clans, and beat the *snot* out of them."

"Nope," I said instantly. "Like that's even a real option! What's your second idea?"

Wyatt clenched his jaw, but continued. "You and I go undercover as a red and green ninja. We'll sneak into the ninja clan and take it over from the inside."

"Because it's *that* easy," I said sarcastically.

"Fine," Wyatt said. "So that leaves my third idea – we figure out who the leaders of the ninja clans are, and then set a trap for them. When we catch 'em, we'll steal *their* masks and humiliate 'em by covering them in syrup and feathers!"

"Where would we get the feathers?" I asked, actually curious.

"From pillows, dummy!" Wyatt said, lightly slapping

74

my arm with the back of his hand.

"While that *does* sound amazing," I said, "I'm pretty sure it's also a terrible idea. But I'm going to steal that syrup and feather prank for myself and get Brayden or Slug with it someday."

Wyatt slouched forward. "Alright then, what do *you* think we should do?"

"I don't know," I answered honestly. "Maybe… we should find them and *talk* to them about what's happening."

"Oh, yeah?" Wyatt said. "And what're you gonna say? Please stop messing with us?"

I paused. "Yeah."

"But what if their plan *isn't* to mess with us," Wyatt said. "What if they're up to something else? Something bigger and badder?"

It made sense. With all the crazy things I'd been through, most of the time those things had nothing to do with *me*. There was always a different goal. The hairs on my arms stood on end when I realized that.

"Where do they train?" I said, still watching the rest of my team.

"No clue," Wyatt said. "We used to be in the overgrown greenhouse at the center of the school, but when I checked there this morning, it was empty."

"You checked already?" I asked.

"Duh-doy," Wyatt said like a little child.

"Then the first thing we have to do is figure out where they're hiding," I said.

Wyatt tapped his fingers on the back of the chair and swayed like he was dancing to music I couldn't hear. He was excited.

"They could be anywhere in the school," I said. "This building is like a flippin' maze with all kinds of hidden hallways and tunnels. But the question is *how* do we find them?"

"Let's make *them* find *us*," Wyatt suggested.

"I like that," I said. "Okay, so how?"

"Bait," Wyatt said.

"Okaaaay…" I said, suddenly uneasy.

"We'll use *you* as bait," he said with a smirk.

"Uuuugh," I groaned as Wyatt stepped away to work out the plans with Olivia. "What have I gotten myself into?"

75

### Wednesday. 7:00 AM. The lobby.

It was early. And cold. And again, I was in school *before* it started.

After I stepped into the lobby, I stopped to blow hot air into my hands.

Principal Davis and my homeroom teacher, Mrs. Robinson, were walking out of the front offices. Mrs. Robinson had a batch of black balloons that floated above her head.

The two adults were far enough away that all I could hear were their mumbles as they spoke to each other. When they saw me, they smiled and waved.

I returned the smile, but not the wave.

"Greetings," a girl's voice said from the corner of the lobby.

Spinning on my heels, I saw Olivia on a bench.

Normal kids don't say "greetings" when they want to say hi, but Olivia wasn't exactly normal.

Popping to her feet, Olivia said, "Wyatt seeks your presence."

See? Who talked like that?

"Uh, yeah, I know," I said. "We were supposed to meet.

76

Where is he?"

"I'll take you to him," she said as she started down the hall.

Uneasy. That's how I felt about the whole thing. Wyatt found his way onto my team. And now he was *seeking* my presence. It was like he was giving me orders.

Olivia stopped at a door next to the elevator. I'd never see the door before in my life even though I walked by it a million times a day.

Pulling the door open, Olivia bobbed her head toward it, gesturing me to go in first.

I took one more look to see if anyone was in the hallways, not to make sure we were alone, but to make sure someone was a witness to the last place Chase Cooper had been seen.

There was nobody.

"You go first," I said.

"No," Olivia said. "It's only polite to allow you to go first. I only wish to be in your favor."

"Stop talking like that!" I said.

Olivia said nothing as she waited for me to go first.

Holding my breath, I stepped into the mysterious room.

Once inside, I found out that it wasn't a room, but a long corridor. The walls were gray bricks and the floor was smooth concrete, which made it look like an unfinished basement. It was like the dungeon, but not underground.

"What is this?" I asked Olivia.

She stepped past me. "The blood vessels of Buchanan. These hallways give people access to any part of the school. It's in case of an emergency. Kids in certain parts of the school will be able to get out faster through here."

"Secret hallways," I repeated. "This school's got everything."

Olivia looked over her shoulder. "And you haven't even scratched the surface yet."

"You mean there's more?" I asked, following Olivia as she turned down one of the corners.

"Oh, yeah," she said, running her fingers along the gray bricks. "You think you know the secrets of Buchanan School? Hardly."

I wasn't sure whether to be excited or scared at that thought.

Olivia stopped at the end of the hallway, where it opened up to a large room.

At the center of the room was a short brick wall that formed a circle on the floor. At one point in time it must've been used as a well. The top of the well was boarded up though, so there wasn't any danger of Timmy falling down it.

Get it? Timmy? Lassie? No? Kay, moving on…

Wyatt was sitting on the side of the well. "Chase, old friend! I'm glad you could make it."

I shuddered when he called me "old friend."

"What d'you mean you're glad I could make it?" I said. "We *agreed* to meet."

"I know, I know," Wyatt said, patting at the air with both hands. "I'm just sayin' that I'm glad you're here."

Instead of sitting next to Wyatt, I leaned against the cold brick wall near the entrance. "I'm here," I said. "What's the plan?"

"The plan is to use you as bait," Wyatt said.

"Right, I already know that," I said. "But *how?*"

Wyatt sighed with a worried look on his face. His forehead wrinkled as his eyebrows tightened. "Good question… I guess we could put you on a pedestal in the lobby. Maybe make a game of it? Throw a bunch of baseballs at a target. If you hit the target, Chase falls into a pool of water?"

"Seriously?" I said.

"You're right," Wyatt said. "Needlessly complicated."

"Ya think?" Olivia said from the entrance.

"Babe," Wyatt said. "You know my love language is words, and when you make sarcastic comments like that, it hurts my feelings."

Olivia's eyes softened. "Sorry, baby. Smooches!" she said, blowing a kiss to Wyatt.

Wyatt bobbed back and forth, and then he caught the invisible kiss. He smiled as he put it in his front pocket.

OMG. Watching Wyatt and Olivia have a moment… If it was possible for a brain to barf, then mine was about ten seconds away from doing it. Puke was going to shoot out of my *ears*.

Olivia smiled. "Good luck," she said as she left Wyatt and me alone.

"Is she gonna help?" I asked.

Wyatt shook his head. "No, she said she had something else to do."

"What?" I said.

"Talk to a teacher about homework or something? I dunno," Wyatt said.

I pushed myself off the wall. "Let's just think simple, okay? We don't know where they're training, but we know they've got eyes all over the school."

"Probably," Wyatt said. He snapped his fingers as an idea popped into his head. "How about you run around the hallways wearing your ninja mask? Those kids are probably always looking for *you*, right?"

For a second, I wanted to argue that it was an idiotic idea, but it actually wasn't. I couldn't think of a better, simpler way to get the red or green ninja clan to come after me.

Finally, I nodded. "Fine."

"Good," Wyatt said, standing from the well at the center of the room. "Then let's go catch us some ninjas!"

### Wednesday. 7:20 AM. The dungeon.

Several minutes later, I was on my own in the lower level of the school, better known as "the dungeon" because it was always cold, and wet, and gross.

I'm gonna go ahead and be honest with you... I wasn't *not* scared.

Double negative. Boom.

Being alone in the dungeon was as scary as running through the woods at two in the morning. When it's packed with kids, it wasn't bad, but when it was empty? Every small noise screamed at you to run for your life.

The creepy buzzing lights didn't help either. Some of them were even burned out, which meant walking in a few feet of almost total darkness.

"Stupid, stupid, stupid," I sang to myself, trying to keep a jolly melody.

A locker slammed from somewhere. I spun around, sure that I was going to see a monster come at me, but I was still alone.

Most of the doors were locked since even teachers stayed out of the dungeon until the very last second possible when their classes started.

I took my ninja mask from my hood and slipped it over my face.

Step by step, I made my way deeper into the dungeon. Once I turned the corner, the light from the stairwell was gone, and I was at the point of no return.

THE
DUNGEON
WHERE NIGHTMARES ARE BORN.
TRUST ME, NEWBORN BABY
NIGHTMARES ARE THE
WORST!

The hallway lights in front of me were worse than the ones back at the stairs. Most of them were busted, leaving the hallway drenched in black shadows.

I was beginning to regret *everything*.

Something behind me touched the floor, barely making any sound, like someone had dropped a towel or something.

I froze, leaning against the lockers. Slowly, I turned to see what was behind me, doing my best to stay calm.

Nothing was there.

The noise came again… and then again… and then again and again, getting closer, but there wasn't anything in the hallway!

And my legs! My legs forgot how to be legs. They were

doing their impression of tree trunks!

My teeth were grinding in my skull as the sounds came closer. I was in the middle of a nightmare!

My voice stopped in my throat as I stared at the empty hallway. Finally, I managed to squeeze out, "C'mon!"

And then, like a videogame, my legs unpaused, and I was sprinting away from the noises as fast as my thin legs could take me.

But the muffled pads hitting the floor behind me kept up. It only made sense that Wyatt's plan worked, and that the monster in the dark was actually a ninja.

With every hallway I turned down, I ran faster. The footsteps chasing me turned into *many* footsteps. Player three had entered the game.

Ahead and to my right was a door that was left wide open. It was the only door in the dungeon that hadn't been locked shut, so I did what any sixth grade ninja would do… I dove in headfirst.

Lucky for me, the room was empty. Unlucky for me, there was only *one* way out of it, and that was back through the door I had just entered.

Sliding under the teacher's desk, I tucked myself away, hoping the ninjas would walk past me. If they did, then I'd have a chance at escaping back through the door.

And if they didn't? Well, I could see the headlines now… "*Sixth Grader Chase Cooper Disappears. Nobody Cares.*"

At the front of the room, I saw the shadows of two ninjas. These guys always traveled in packs of two or three.

Watching the ninjas enter the room, I sat completely still under the teacher's desk. My heart was pounding so hard that it felt like it was trying to escape from my chest.

There was a red ninja and a green one. They were totes working together.

So much for the plan. I was supposed to lure the ninjas out of hiding so Wyatt and I could figure out where they were training. Instead, I was cowering under a desk, hoping that the bell would ring.

"Where'd he go?" the first ninja said. It was a boy.

"I don't know. Is there another way out?" the other ninja said. A girl.

"Not that I see."

"Lemme turn the light on."

"No! We work in the dark. *Always* in the dark."

"*Actually* that's pretty bad for your eyes," the girl said with attitude.

"There you go again! This is why everyone calls you '*Actually*' instead of your real name! Because you're forever correcting people with *facts*."

"Wait…" the girl said. "What's that?"

"What's what?"

"*That*… under the teacher's desk," she answered.

Oh noes…

Their footsteps got closer and closer.

I had no choice. I rolled out from the desk and ran straight for the front door, but in my confusion, I had accidentally ran to the *back* of the room.

"There!" the girl shouted. "He's cornering himself!"

"Noob!" the other ninja shouted.

I slammed into the back wall. My arms were caught up in long strings that wrapped themselves around my hands. I didn't know what was going on, but it couldn't have been good.

The red and green ninjas slid to a stop.

I stared at their shadows, trying to get myself untangled from whatever weird web I was caught in.

"He's not alone," the boy said.

The girl ninja took a step backward. "Well played, Chase... you think you can trick the two of us, but we're *smarter* than that. We *know* when we're *outnumbered*."

Outnumbered? What the heck was that girl talking about?

The two ninjas ran back to the door, sliding across desks, and doing cartwheels to show off.

At the door, the girl ninja turned around. From the lights in the hallway, I saw that her ninja outfit was green. "We'll meet again, Chase. And when we do, we'll bring more of *our* friends."

The green ninja raised a small ball, and then she slammed it into the floor. A cloud of chalk dust burst at her feet. When the fog lifted, she was gone.

I leaned my head back, bumping it against the wall. I was alone again, but that time I was happy to be.

The strings around my hands and arms tugged at something above my head.

"Hello?" Wyatt said from the doorway like he had teleported there.

"Dude," I said. "Did you see the other ninjas out there?"

Wyatt leaned back and scanned the halls. "Nope. No one else out here."

Was it a coincidence that Wyatt appeared so quickly after the other ninjas disappeared? Or was I just being paranoid?

"Wait," he paused. "I thought we said you were gonna come down here alone."

"I *am* alone," I said, still against the back wall.

"No, you're not," Wyatt said, stepping through the door. "You got, like, five ninjas behind you!"

"What're talking about?" I asked, annoyed. "There's nobody else in here except for you and me!"

"And the five ninjas standing behind you," Wyatt said, flipping on the light.

I squeezed my eyes shut because the lights hurt them.

84

"Oh, my bad," Wyatt said. "You *are* alone."

Forcing my eyelids open, I looked at the strings of ribbon that were wrapped around my arms. They led to five black balloons that floated right next to my head.

On the whiteboard at the front of the room was a message that read, "*Happy 40th Birthday, Mr. Lopez!*" A cake covered in black frosting sat on top of his desk. The black balloons were part of his "over the hill" party.

I freed myself from the clutches of the evil balloons, and then took my mask off. "I got cornered in here. Those ninjas must've thought these black balloons were my other ninjas."

Wyatt snorted. "I thought they were too. Those black balloons looked like ninja masks in the dark."

"I got super lucky then," I said.

"But hey!" Wyatt said, grinning. "Our plan worked! You got their attention!"

My blood boiled. "It didn't work at all, dude! I got them to chase me, but we still don't know where they're hiding!"

"Fine," Wyatt said. "Maybe it didn't turn out the way we..."

I looked at Wyatt. "The way we what?"

Wyatt didn't answer. He was staring at a spot on the floor next to the door.

I wasn't sure what caught his attention.

Kneeling down, Wyatt slid his hand across the linoleum. "Look at all these tiny pebbles," he said, pinching some of them in his fingers.

The pebbles were small, and they were speckled black and gray.

"This might not have been pointless after all," Wyatt said. "Looks like we just found a solid clue."

"You're just gonna take that back to the lab," I said sarcastically. "Study it under a microscope, and then cross reference the evidence to figure out which quarry it came from?"

I had no idea what I was saying. I was trying to sound

like the detective shows my dad always watched.

"If you'd rather be bait again…" Wyatt trailed off waiting for my answer.

"No, no!" I said. "Clues are good! I'm all *about* clues, dude! Let's go figure out where those clues came from!"

If studying clues meant I didn't have to get hunted by a bunch of ninjas, then I was gonna study clues like it was my job.

### Wednesday. 11:35 AM. Lunch.

I spent the rest of the morning looking over my shoulder every couple seconds. It sounds crazy, but when you have to worry about ninjas sneak attacking you, checking every couple seconds might not even be enough.

Stepping out of the kitchen, I scanned the cafeteria for my friends. I didn't have much of an appetite so all I got was a juice and a chocolate chip cookie.

"Outta the way, mouthbreather!" Gidget's voice joked.

I stepped aside to let Gidget through. She had a bottle of water in one hand, and her cell phone in the other, still typing away with one thumb. She wasn't even looking at the screen! She'd win gold in the Olympics if there was a texting event.

Naomi was next to her. My brain was so cluttered that I didn't even notice they were in line behind me.

"What's up with you?" Naomi asked, carrying her lunch tray.

"We said your name a billion times in there," Gidget said, nodding back to the kitchen. "You totes ignored us."

"I didn't mean to," I said. "I think... I've just got a lot on my mind."

"The robot?" Gidget asked.

"Or is it about Wyatt?" Naomi said.

"It's both," I said.

I think Naomi could tell I was stressed and didn't really want to talk about it because she changed the subject. "Cookies and juice? Lunch of champions, right?"

I let out a small laugh. "You're probably right, but when I want chocolate, I gotta get it."

"Right?" Gidget said.

I looked at her bottle of water. "Where's your food?" I asked. "It's weird seeing you without fries."

"I just feel like nibbling today," Gidget said.

That meant she was going to take bits of other people's food like everyone's lunch was part of her own personal buffet. None of us cared that she did it though.

Gidget stepped past me and walked down the side of the cafeteria. "C'mon, our team's already at a table."

Naomi and I followed behind her.

"So..." Naomi paused. "What's bothering you?"

Naomi was the kind of friend who didn't pull punches. And by that, I meant she never danced around the hard questions. If she disagreed with you, she'd tell you. If she had a problem with something you were doing, she'd tell you. If you looked like life was beating you down, she'd ask how she could help you.

I really liked that about her.

"I'm not sure," I sighed. "Maybe it's Wyatt. Maybe it's the robot. Maybe it's Olivia tagging along everywhere."

"Where's *everywhere?*" Naomi asked. "She was only with us last night."

I forgot that my ninja clan didn't know I met with Wyatt earlier that morning. I thought it best to keep it that way... at least for a little longer.

"No," I said. "I meant last night. She's prob'ly gonna be everywhere now that Wyatt's on the team."

A light bulb clicked in Naomi's head. "You're working with him on something else, aren't you?"

"No! I mean, yes!" I said, not sure which answer I was going to go with. And then I surprised myself. "Yeah, we're kind of checking out some things."

"I think you're putting a little too much trust in Wyatt."

"No, I'm keeping my distance. It's just that... I mean, he's kind of being cool right now, and there *are* things he can help with."

"What're you guys up to?"

"I don't want to say anything yet. At least not until I have a little more information."

"More information on what, Chase? Did you forget that I used to be a Scavenger? Did you forget that I know secrets about kids that would make their mothers weep?"

"No, I didn't forget."

"Then tell me what you guys are doing. You need someone you can trust to keep you grounded."

I said nothing.

"Whatever, dude," Naomi smiled. "I'll just have to be your secret guardian ninja then. I got your back from the shadows. I promise."

"You don't have to—" I said.

Naomi interrupted me, making her serious adult face. "You can *trust* me, Chase. I made my mistakes and I vowed never to make them again."

"I know," I said, finally reaching the spot where the rest of Team Cooper was sitting. "I need to get a little more info before I want to say anything else."

I couldn't tell if Naomi was frustrated or hurt. "Kay," was all that she said before taking the spot next to Gidget.

Zoe, Faith, Brayden, and Slug were sitting quietly. Olivia was at the other end of the table right next to Wyatt, who was in the middle of telling a story.

"...so I turned the guitar amp off and got out of there as *fast* as I could!" Wyatt said.

Laughter exploded from the rest of the team. Wyatt's story must have been a funny one.

"What happened after that?" Brayden asked.

"They called my parents," Wyatt said, "but I never got in trouble for it. They figured I was a kid bein' a kid. I got a stern talkin' to from my parents because it *was* at a *funeral*, but I never got grounded or anything."

"Man," Slug said. "My parents never spanked me, but I'd *totes* get spanked if I ever did that."

Wyatt chuckled, wiping a tear from his eye. And then he pointed at Brayden with both his hands. "Hey, dude, my dad said it was cool if we used his four wheeler to go monster hunting sometime. He said it's fine as long as we don't ride after dark."

Brayden slapped the table. "*Awesoooooome!*"

Everyone was laughing at Wyatt's stories? Brayden and Wyatt had a monster hunting date? What the heck was happening?

I dropped my cookie on the table and sat on the other side of Naomi.

Wyatt went on with another embarrassing story, making my friends laugh until their sides hurt. Zoe was in tears.

And I wasn't sure what I was feeling. I *wanted* Wyatt to join the team. I *wanted* to give him another chance at *not being a jerk.* I *wanted* my friends to make him feel welcome.

So why was I so uncomfortable with it?

Wyatt leaned back in his chair, and then did the two handed point again, but this time it was at Slug. "Hey, I'm makin' corndogs in the science lab tonight. How many should I put you down for? Two? Three?"

"Dude, make it five," Slug said. "And one pillow 'cause I'll be takin' a corndog nap afterward."

"You got it, brah," Wyatt said and then looked at everyone else. "Corndogs with a side of mac and cheese while we work! Sounds perfect!"

My friends nodded, talking about how much fun it was going to be.

Yep. I was definitely uncomfortable with it.

**Wednesday. 2:50 PM. The science lab.**

I'm happy to say that I didn't see any other holiday ninjas for the rest of the day. And trust me, I was looking.

I was sitting in the science lab, waiting for the rest of my team to join me because none of them were there yet. It wasn't like any of them to be late to anything, especially Zoe, but there I was... sitting alone.

Carlyle's team was behind their cloth partition singing more jolly sounding pirate songs, swaying back and forth so hard that it felt like the floor was bouncing. How were they able to get *any* work done? They spent all their time acting like a buncha dizzy pirates!

Every now and again, the sound of a hammer clinking came from Carlyle's corner, but it wasn't from them working. It was in tune with the beat of one of their chanteys.

*Ugh! Stinkin' pirates!*

A loud crash came from Dante's corner. I sat perfectly still, watching his shadow completely spaz out again over his robot. He was kicking and pushing the machine, yelling harsh things because it wouldn't work.

"That kid..." I whispered. "Wow. Just... wow."

I heard Carlyle laugh loudly. I couldn't help myself. I

poked my head out from behind the bed sheet and looked at the pirate's section of the room.

In front of Carlyle were all the parts for their robot scattered across the floor. One of his pirate buddies was looking over the different pieces. He was like confused dog, tilting his head, baffled by the strange objects.

Another pirate had a tricycle that he rode in small circles like he was part of some kind of pirate circus or something.

At the edge of their circle was something that looked like an empty container. It was huge too. At least, huger than the robot my team was building.

And yeah, huger *is* a word. I just added it to the dictionary. Don't look though. It'll take time for it to update... and stuff.

It was Wednesday, and Carlyle's team hadn't even started building their robot!

The door to the science lab swung open, and Wyatt walked through. My entire team was behind him, listening to another one of his stories.

Olivia was the last through the door. She dragged way behind because of Brayden's cologne. Once she was in the room, she took the same seat several feet away, just out of noseshot of Brayden's musk.

"Right?" Wyatt said, flipping a chair around as usual. "If

93

they didn't want kids crawling on those dinosaur fossils, then they shoulda put a sign up!"

"Dude," Slug said. "You. Are. Insane!"

"Nah," Wyatt said. "You woulda done the same thing if you were there."

Zoe giggled like a schoolgirl with a crush.

Wyatt eyeballed me with a smile on his face. I couldn't tell if it was a villainous smile or not, but I couldn't shake the feeling that letting him on the team might've been a mistake.

Naomi knew I was upset. She never said anything though, probably because she didn't want to bring it up in front of everyone.

"You guys are late," I said.

I wasn't angry about it. I was just worried that we had a ton of work to do still.

Wyatt spoke for everyone. "Sorry, man. Remember how I said I wanted to make corndogs in here? Well, the lunch staff wouldn't let me bring a fryer into this room. Makes sense really. So I had to make 'em in the kitchen. We're all late because we were eating."

Slug leaned back, yawning. "I'm stuffed."

"You guys didn't invite me?" I said, my voice cracking slightly.

"Tried to find you, but couldn't," Wyatt said.

"I would've texted you," Gidget said. "But I totes forgot."

I didn't know what to say.

Slug snorted loudly as he slid to the floor. He was taking the corndog nap he talked about.

Wyatt got up from his seat, suddenly holding a knitted blanket. I had no idea where he got the blanket, but once again, I wasn't surprised. He placed it over Slug and said, "Shhhhh, this little guy's pooped. Let him get some rest."

Oh.

My.

Corndog.

Was it possible that it was still Monday morning? And that I was still dreaming somehow? I pinched myself on the arm to find out.

It hurt like crazy.

Nope. Not a dream.

We only had one more day to work on our project after

that, which meant our robot needed to be almost completed by the end of that day. It'd be even better if we were able to finish it before we left.

Zoe and Faith were hard at work with the guts of the robot. It wasn't much, but Dr. Tenderfoot said it didn't need to be.

They attached the battery pack to the "stomach" of the robot, which was then plugged into a small gearbox that was connected to what I guess would be the robot's shoulders.

Then the gearbox turned the main gear, which was supposed to rotate the robot's hand and make it look like it was waving. At the top of the robot was a light bulb.

Gidget and Faith took it a step further and connected a small metal shaft to the robot's side and wrist. Their hope was that the main gear would turn and move two parts at the same time, pushing the arm up and waving simultaneously.

If it worked, then it meant the whole thing moved simply because *one* gear was rotating at the shoulder.

Pretty crazy if you asked me.

Slug and Brayden were putting the finishing touches on the shell of the robot, to give it that extra boost of "cool."

Except the shell they made looked like a giant cow.

"What's that supposed to be?" Faith asked.

"A cow!" Brayden said proudly.

I guess they *wanted* it to look like a cow.

"Can't you tell?" Brayden asked.

"Sorta," Faith answered, walking slowly around the shell. "I mean, it could be a cow from, like, a nightmare or something."

Zoe perked up. "Oh, nightmare cow! Gotta remember to tell Brody about that. He'll wanna call dibs on it for a band name." Zoe placed her finger on her chin and spoke quietly. "With a name like that, they'd have to be a death metal band though…"

"It's not like I got much help from Slug," Brayden continued, nudging the sleeping kid on the floor.

Slug snorted, but kept right on sleeping. His arms and legs moved like he was a dog running in his dream.

"Slug's chasing squirrels," Gidget said.

"I think it looks great," Naomi said.

"Thanks!" Brayden said.

"The competition's not based on appearances anyway,"

Naomi added. "So it's not like we'll get points taken away based on how *ugly* something is."

Brayden made a face. "...thanks?"

"Naomi's right, you guys," Wyatt said. "We just gotta make this thing work. That's all that matters."

"Oh, it's *gonna* work," Faith said confidently. "Let's *do* this."

Zoe looked at everyone with an excited smile. She placed her finger on the switch under the robot. "Three... two... one..."

Everyone held their breath. Zoe flipped the switch.

And then nothing happened.

Zoe scrunched her nose and then flipped the switch back and forth rapidly.

The robot didn't do anything.

"C'mon," Zoe said. "Work!"

"We did everything right!" Faith said. "We had the gears working before we bolted it on!"

Wyatt leaned closer to the robot, inspecting the small battery pack. And then he pressed his finger on top.

Everyone jumped back because the robot sprung forward, alive and moving the way Zoe and Faith had planned. The arm moved up and down while the hand spun in a circle, waving like it was a model in a robot parade. The light bulb at the top of the robot was shining brightly.

Zoe laughed, wiping some sweat from her brow. She was more nervous than she let on.

"It was just a bad connection!" Wyatt said. He took his finger off the battery pack and the robot stopped moving. "All we have to do is screw that part down a little tighter and it'll be good. We could prob'ly get away with just using a little tape."

I sat back in my seat and felt relieved. "Team Cooper's gonna win this thing! That robot is so flippin' sweet! I even *like* how it's gonna look like an ugly cow!"

"Hey!" Brayden said. "It might be ugly on the outside, but she's beautiful on the inside!"

"That's all that counts," Wyatt said. "What should we name it?"

"Hup-Hup," Faith said.

"I like it," I said. "Hup-Hup, the robot."

"We're gonna be rich!" Wyatt said. Apparently he still thought the prize was going to be a million dollars.

The whole team was excited.

Even Olivia was smiling from her chair. She had her cell phone out and was taking pictures of our robot.

We were about 99% finished, and we were *still* a whole day early!

All the junk that bothered me about Wyatt disappeared because we had brought Hup-Hup to life. Even Olivia sitting in the corner was fine with me.

Adding him to the team was a risk, but it turned out to be a good thing. He was making everyone laugh and work together. Maybe there was a reason he was always the leader of a ninja clan – because *maybe* he was a good leader. Or maybe he just knew how to get kids to work together.

"Alright, guys," Wyatt said. "This calls for a *proper* celebration. Tonight. My house. Seven o'clock. Pizza is on me."

"Boom!" Slug said, snapping to attention. "Bring on the pizza! Wait... what're we talkin' about? Where am I? Why do I taste hot dogs?"

"Give him a minute," Gidget said.

After a second, Slug stretched his arms out and drifted back to sleep.

"He'll be in and out for the rest of the night," Gidget said. "He'll wake up around midnight and complain about how he can't sleep. Then he'll play videogames until about four or five in the morning. Then he'll sleep like a brick until it's time to go to school."

"Livin' the dream," Brayden said.

Wyatt pointed at me. "Alright, guys. I'll text all of you my address, and then I'll see you tonight. Cool?"

My friends, my *best* friends all nodded, talking to each other about how cool it was going to be. Wyatt went around the circle, programming everyone's number into his phone. I suddenly felt uneasy as I watched him do it.

I couldn't put my finger on why it all bothered me again, but all I knew was that it did. Maybe it was my own problem. Maybe I was just being a little too suspicious when it wasn't necessary.

Oh well. I shrugged it off.

Besides, there were bigger things to think about, like getting our robot to actually work! Celebrating at Wyatt's house might be weird, but at least we were *celebrating* something.

I was just glad we weren't spending the rest of the night frustrated the way Dante was probably going to do.

I looked at Dante's side of the room to see how he was holding up, but he was already gone.

**Wednesday. 7:10 PM. Wyatt's house.**

I had never been to Wyatt's house, and to be honest, I really had no idea where he lived. When I looked up the address on the Internet, I found out that he only lived a couple miles away.

I know it sounds crazy that I had no idea Wyatt lived so close to me, but I'll tell you exactly why – he lived in a neighborhood totally different than mine.

His house... was a mansion. And his neighbor's houses? They were mansions too.

Wyatt lived in a rich neighborhood that I never bothered to explore on my bike. Brayden and I always rode by his street but the dirty looks the old people gave were enough to keep us away.

There were times when life slapped me across the forehead, and made me realize the world was much bigger than what I saw.

Let me put this in videogame terms. When I go to the mall, the other shoppers are NPCs, or non-playable characters. They don't affect anything I'm doing. Basically, they're just movements in the background and mean nothing to me. I'll never see them again in my *whole* entire life.

But to them? *I'm* the NPC. I'm *nothing* in their lives – just a passing human that they might or might not have seen and will probably never see again.

I guess what I'm trying to say is that seeing Wyatt's house made me realize he *wasn't* just a non-playable character.

Nobody was. We were all on our own mission, passing other people who were on *their* own mission.

I know, right? I usually have to take a nap after my brain thinks that much.

Team Cooper was at Wyatt's dinner table. Small pizzas lined the center of the table. Each one had a couple slices missing. It looked like a pizza buffet.

And the pizzas smelled amazing.

HEY... DOESN'T THIS PICTURE MAKE YOU HUNGRY FOR PIZZA? WYATT'S HOUSE FOR PIZZA

When I walked in, Team Cooper was in the middle of a weird conversation.

"Whatever, dude," Zoe said. "You can believe what you want, but it's just not possible."

"It's *totes* possible!" Slug said defensively. "Just 'cause you can't see it in your brain doesn't mean it *wasn't* happening!"

"You seriously believe that?" Zoe said. "I know it's widely accepted by all of humanity at his point, but I *don't* believe *everybody* was kung fu fighting. Everybody means *all* the people."

"Agree to disagree then," Slug said, folding his arms.

Zoe shook her head, laughing.

The oven timer chirped from across the room.

"Gidget, this one's yours," Wyatt said, pulling an oven mitt over his hand. "Spinach artichoke comin' right up."

"Hey, Chase," Zoe said. "I had Wyatt make a buffalo chicken pizza for you. It's crazy spicy though."

Buffalo chicken pizza was my new favorite thing ever. I always thought pizzas were meat, cheese, and pizza sauce until I tasted my first buffalo chicken pizza. It's chopped up chicken spread out across a layer of buffalo wing sauce and then blanketed with mozzarella cheese.

Zoe set a slice on a plate and put it in front of the empty seat next to her.

Brayden leaned over the kitchen counter top, inspecting all the ingredients Wyatt had set out in different dishes. "Man, you're hardcore about cooking, huh?"

Wyatt smiled. "My dad's a professional chef."

"That's awesome," Brayden said.

I took a huge honkin' bite of my buffalo chicken pizza. The crust was soft and kept warm by the piping hot buffalo wing sauce on top. The chicken was so tender that it almost melted in my mouth. And the cheese? I couldn't tell what was different about the cheese...

"You're tasting the bleu cheese, aren't you?" Wyatt said, setting down Gidget's spinach artichoke special delivery on the table.

Pushing the food to the side of my mouth, I spoke. "This is what bleu cheese tastes like?"

"Yup!" Wyatt said, dusting the flour off his hands. "Tastes like angel wings that fell from the skies."

"Chew with your mouth shut," Zoe said, embarrassed for me.

"OMG," Gidget sighed. "I think I'm gonna *marry* this spinach artichoke pizza!"

Olivia was creating another pizza back by the ingredients bar. I was getting used to her being around, but it was getting kind of weird that she didn't talk much. Brayden still smelled like a lumberjack, which was probably why she stayed at a distance.

I inhaled the rest of my pizza and grabbed another slice.

There was even a mac and cheese pizza that Faith was guarding with her life. She didn't just take a slice of it either. She had the *entire* pizza in front of her, eating it with a fork. "This," she kept joking. "This one's *mine*."

Slug was awake, but it didn't look like he would be for long. On his plate were eight crusts – *just* the crusts. They were the only remaining parts left of his pizza eating rampage.

Naomi only had one slice that she was eating. It wasn't anything special – just a slice of regular old pepperoni.

Zoe leaned closer to me and spoke quietly. "Wyatt's really turned a new leaf, hasn't he?"

I only nodded because I was chewing.

"What do you think?" she asked. "Could this all be part of some kinda larger scheme?"

I shrugged my shoulders.

Zoe sighed. "I really hope this new version of him is for real."

"It'd make life a lot easier, that's for sure," I said after swallowing.

"For everyone," Naomi added.

"He told me he wanted to be in our ninja clan," Slug said.

"Nope," I said. "Being on our team is one thing, but I have to draw the line somewhere. We *used* to be in a ninja clan together. Didn't work out so well."

Slug's comment should've bothered me more, but I honestly didn't care. It's not like I was going to let him be in my ninja clan anyway, so there was nothing to worry about.

Everyone devoured the rest of the pizza while joking and sharing crazy stories with each other. All in all, Wyatt's party didn't turn out to be as bad as I thought it would be.

Wyatt brought out a bunch of board games to end the night with. He set them on the table and said that Zoe got to choose which one we played since she was the class president.

It was as if Wyatt had finally won everyone over.

Once I cleared my plate, I took it to the sink to rinse it off.

Wyatt followed me over. He leaned back, folded his

102

arms, and spoke under his breath. "So those pebbles... I figured it out."

Olivia had taken the spot on the other side of me.

I glanced over my shoulder to make sure everyone was still at a distance. They were, but I turned the sink on so nobody would hear us talk. "You know where the pebbles came from?"

Wyatt nodded. "I had a hunch when we first found them, but I didn't wanna say nothin' until I knew for sure."

"So?" I asked. "Where?"

"The roof of the school," Wyatt said. "That's why they were speckled black and gray."

"Those kids train on the roof?" I said, a little shocked.

"I doubt they're training," Wyatt said. "They'd make too much noise if they were training. They're probably just having meetings up there."

"Actually," Olivia said, "the roof is solid enough that you probably couldn't hear an elephant stomp around up there."

"Welp," Wyatt said. "There's really only one way to find out."

"Find out what?" Naomi said, nudging me aside to put her plate into the sink.

"Um," I said, hesitating. There wasn't any point in keeping Naomi or my other ninjas in the dark anymore. "Wyatt thinks some new ninjas are meeting on the roof at Buchanan."

"I *knew* it!" Naomi said with a scowl. "I *knew* you two were doing ninja things behind everyone's back!"

"It wasn't behind everyone's back," I said. "I wanted to wait until we had more before coming to you guys."

"You *always* say that," Naomi said.

"So what's the game plan?" Wyatt asked me.

I answered Wyatt with another question. "What happens if we find them there? It's not like we're going to do anything. I'm *not* fighting anyone because, one, it's stupid, and two, they outnumber us by a billion to two."

"But we can't do *nothing*," Wyatt said.

"I know," I said, frustrated.

"Let's just check it out," Wyatt suggested. "If they're there, we'll try to talk to them. If they're not, there's nothing to worry about."

"Just talk to them?" Naomi said. "About what? Life? Love? What we all wanna be when we grow up?"

"Naomi's right," I said. "It's not like we can tell them to quit bein' ninjas."

Wyatt clenched his teeth. We were getting on his nerves. "Those kids can go play ninjas all they want somewhere else! Someone took my ninja clan, and I'm gonna take it back."

"Babe," Olivia said. "Calm down a little."

Wyatt took a breath. "Look, those kids are up to something. You *know* it. We *all* know it! We just don't know *what* it is. And to be frank, I don't wanna know! I wanna stop it before it even happens!"

"Okay, *Frank*," Naomi said, smiling.

Wyatt gave her a dirty look. "I've missed you, Naomi," he said sarcastically. "You're a real breath of fresh air, but only if you're *into* breathing fresh air."

Naomi and I looked at each other. Neither one of us could tell if the "fresh air" thing was a burn or not.

I hated the thought that the red and green ninjas had a bigger picture they were painting. They were building up to something. We just didn't know what.

"Okay," I said. "Let's meet tomorrow morning. Early. We'll check out the roof, but that's *all* we're gonna do. We're not gonna talk to them. They won't even know we're there. The only reason we're doing this is to see if that's *actually* where they're meeting."

Wyatt nodded. "At least we're moving in the right direction."

"I'll let the other guys know," Naomi said.

"Really?" Wyatt snipped. "Why do *they* need to know?"

"Because they're part of my ninja clan," I said. "And they're my friends. They're with us whether you like it or not."

Wyatt tightened his lips. "Fine," he whispered.

### Thursday. 7:25 AM. The lobby.

Brayden, Naomi, Gidget, and Slug were filled in after Wyatt's party. I told them everything that happened with the red and green ninjas, and how Wyatt was booted from his ninja clan. I told them all about stealing my mask and how there was a new leader for each of those clans, but we didn't know who they were.

I even told them about the balloons in the dungeon, and how they were fooled, thinking the black balloons were members of my ninja clan.

Naomi laughed pretty hard about that. "There's a bunch of those balloons on the cafeteria stage too," she said. "I wondered what they were doing there. I guess they ordered too many."

Once my ninjas were up to date with the *sitch*, they were pumped to help, so we planned on meeting in the lobby before school.

My ninja clan was already waiting when I stepped through the front doors. Wyatt was there too, but Olivia wasn't with him.

"S'up, man?" Brayden said first.

"Stinkin' cold outside!" I said, rubbing my hands

together.

"Normal people wear *winter* clothes during the *winter*," Gidget said, typing something into her phone. "Hashtag, frostbite. Hashtag, Not so smart. Hashtag, actually pretty dumb."

"I get it," I said. "I shoulda worn gloves at least."

Wyatt was standing in front of the elevator. The doors slid open immediately after he pushed the up arrow. "Can we do this now? We're wasting time down here."

"THE SCARIEST MOVIE I'VE EVER SEEN!" -SOME CRITIC
# KIDS IN AN ELEVATOR
COMING SOON TO A THEATER NEAR YOU...NOT REALLY.

All six of us got onto the elevator. We weren't stuffed into it, but there definitely wasn't room to do cartwheels and stuff. Wait... even if there was *one* kid, there wouldn't be room to do cartwheels. Unless that kid was tiny. Like, *super* tiny. Like, six-inches-tall tiny. How cool would that be? A six-inch person could ride all kinds of remote controlled cars and helicopters and—y'know what? Nevermind.

Gidget bobbed her head back and forth to the beat of the elevator music. Even Slug kind of bounced his body up and down, dancing. He had a small bag of chocolate drops in his hand that he shook like a tambourine.

Once the elevator reached the second floor, the doors slid open. Wyatt was the first one out.

"This thing doesn't go straight to the roof?" I asked.

"No," Wyatt said, coldly. It was different from how he had acted all week. "But there's a couple other ways to the roof."

"If it's a ladder, then count me out," Gidget said. "I'm not really in a ladder climbing mood today."

"Baby," Wyatt said.

Gidget glared at Wyatt. Then she held her hand out at him. "Whatever, dude. Talk to the hand."

"Hey, 1990 called," Wyatt said. "They want their insult back."

"Oh yeah?" Gidget fumed. "Well, 2060 called. They said you died and nobody went to your funeral!"

Everyone gasped at Gidget's burn.

She shook her head immediately. "Nope, nope, nope. Too dark. I knew it was too dark the second it left my mouth."

"Anyways... there *is* a ladder, but there's also a staircase," Wyatt said, pulling open a large metal door that led to the stairwell. Again, Wyatt was the first to go through. He was a boy on a mission.

"Wait up, dude!" I said, catching up to Wyatt on the stairs by skipping every other step. "We're just seeing if they're there! That's it!"

Wyatt stopped on the step in front of the door to the roof. "Of course," he said. "I'll be as quiet as a kitten."

And then... Wyatt kicked the door open.

"A really *loud, ninja* kitten," he said after the door slammed open.

There, on the rooftop of Buchanan School, was a herd of holiday ninjas. Kids in red and green ninja costumes clumped together in groups, talking. *Not* training. And I think some of them even had cups of coffee. Were we interrupting an evil ninja business meeting?

"Gimme back my ninja clan!" Wyatt shouted as he stepped through the door.

I should've let him deal with the ninjas by himself, but I just couldn't. I grabbed his arm and pulled him back into the stairwell. The door swung shut on its own, leaving us in quiet darkness.

"So much for staying hidden," Naomi said at the back of the group.

"Does this mean we go back down, or…" Slug said, trailing off. He threw a couple more pieces of chocolate into his mouth.

"Are you crazy?" I said to Wyatt.

"It was *my* clan," Wyatt growled. "And I want it back!"

"You know that you might not get it back, right?" I said. "That was always a possibility!"

"Uh, guys?" Gidget said coolly. "We should prob'ly get goin' now, huh? I mean, there *is* an army of ninjas right outside the door, and they know we're in here."

"Maybe they'll go away," Brayden said.

"Really?" Gidget replied. "You think if we turn the lights off, they'll think nobody's home?"

"Maybe!" Brayden said, slightly panicked.

The doorknob jiggled. I grabbed it and set my foot against the wall, keeping the holiday ninjas from opening the door.

"Just let go!" Wyatt said.

"You got some sorta death wish?" I said. "If I let go, this stairwell gets *flooded* with ninjas, and if that happens, we're toast! Lightly buttered toast!"

"Dudes, real quick," Slug said. "Are chocolate drops supposed to make your mouth burn?"

I'm not sure Slug's mind was completely aware of the situation.

"No," Gidget said to her brother. "They're not."

"Man," Slug said, tilting his head. "I should prob'ly get to the nurse then."

"How are we so different?" Gidget sighed.

"Um, helloooo?" I sang. "We're kind of having a crisis up here!"

"Oh, right," Slug said. "Holiday ninjas and stuff."

The door pushed open slightly. I slammed my whole body into it to keep it shut.

"Get back down the stairs," I said to my ninja clan. "I'll hold the door as long as I can, but it ain't gonna be long!"

Since Naomi was the last in line, she ran to the bottom of the stairs so the others could go down too. I knew she would've stayed if she were right next to me.

Gidget snapped a quick selfie with me in the background. I might've been two seconds away from death, but I still made a dorky face. After that, she and Slug hopped to the bottom of the stairs.

Brayden didn't budge. "I'm not leaving," he said boldly.

"I know," I said.

The door opened about an inch. Brayden grabbed my forearms and helped me pull it back shut. The ninjas on the other side were shouting and pounding on the metal door.

"So what now?" Wyatt asked. "We're just gonna sit here, pullin' the door shut all day long?"

Wyatt was right. At some point, we were gonna have to let go.

"Okay, okay, okay," I said quickly. "On the count of three, we make a break for it."

"Back down the stairs?" Wyatt asked.

"No. Through the door," I said sarcastically. "Yes, down the stairs!"

"You don't need to be like that," Wyatt huffed.

"This is all your fault!" I said. "Kicking the door open

was never part of the plan!"

"Not *your* plan," Wyatt said.

"We were supposed to work together on this!"

"And we are!" Wyatt said. "I'm sorry if I have a habit of working faster than you. That's how I get things done, Chase!"

"Children, please," Brayden said. "Can we all act like grown up kids and focus on what's happening right now?"

The door yanked open again, farther than an inch that time. Brayden and I pulled it back shut.

"There are so many ninjas out there that I can't even see the roof!" Brayden said.

And then Wyatt's angry eyes disappeared. "Okay," he said. "Kicking the door might've been a mistake."

"Ya think?" I said.

"On three?" he asked me.

I nodded and took a deep breath. "One…"

Brayden stared into space, waiting.

"Two…"

Wyatt was also staring at nothing.

"…*three!*"

All three of us spun around to run down the stairs, but the second I let go of the doorknob, it swung open. All at once, the ninjas on the other side spilled into the stairwell, rolling over one another like a landslide of ninjas.

"Watch out!" Wyatt squealed with a super high-pitched voice as he disappeared into the mess of tumbling ninjas.

Brayden reached his hand out to me, but it was too late. We both were sucked into the mass of holiday ninjas. The only thing we could do was ride the wave until we hit the bottom of the stairs.

I didn't know where Naomi, Gidget, and Slug were, but I was glad they managed to get away.

When the world stopped spinning, I found myself on top of a pile of red and green ninjas. They were groaning in pain. My body hurt too, but there wasn't any time for me to rub my sore spots.

I grabbed Brayden's arm and pulled him out of the blob of holiday ninjas.

Wyatt was at the door that led to the hallway, holding it open. "C'mon!" he said. "Before they get up!"

Back at the door to the rooftop, someone shouted, "They're getting away! Go after them!"

The ninjas on the ground heard the order, but they didn't move. They were still nursing their bruised knees and elbows.

Brayden and I wasted no time and dashed through the door Wyatt was holding open.

There were a few kids in the hallway, staring in our direction because Wyatt had slammed the door shut. It was a good thing because it meant the ninjas from the roof wouldn't keep coming after us since there were witnesses.

Naomi, Gidget, and Slug were nowhere to be seen.

"Be cool," Wyatt said.

I tried to straighten up, but it hurt. Instead, I hunched over, keeping a hand on my lower back. Pretty sure I looked like my grandpa.

Brayden was limping next to me. Wyatt put a hand on his shoulder to help him keep balanced, even though Wyatt was trying to walk through a limp of his own.

We all stared at each other for a moment.

And then, because of how redonkulous we looked, we started laughing.

"With a voice like yours, you could be a singer for an

80's hair band," I said to Wyatt.

Wyatt rolled his eyes and faked a laugh. "Bwah ha ha, very funny. My voice gets high when I get excited."

The clock on the wall said we only had a few minutes until school started. There wasn't enough time for us to talk about our next move, so we agreed to meet again during lunch.

Waiting wasn't going to be the hard part. The hard part was going to be figuring out what to do next.

**Thursday. 11:45 AM. Lunch.**

My ninja clan was on the top step of the nook in the lobby. I could see them through the tinted windows that lined one side of the cafeteria. After scarfing down my lunch, I dumped my trash and stepped into the lobby.

Wyatt was sitting with them talking about what happened after they escaped the stairwell. He even pulled his shirt up to show them the bruise he got from tumbling down the stairs.

"Seriously, dude," Gidget said, disgusted. "Put your shirt down."

Olivia stepped out of the cafeteria after I did, walking towards the group. But when she got closer, she started up with her sneezing fit again. She sat on a bench and wiped her nose.

"Stop using that cheap perfume!" she yelled at Brayden from across the lobby.

"It's cologne," Brayden yelled back. "And it was super expensive!"

"It was a waste of money because you smell like a pinecone!" Olivia said.

"*I smell like a man!*" Brayden shouted.

113

Naomi and Gidget giggled. Slug smiled, shaking his head. Wyatt was sitting with his back against the wall, staring angrily at nothing because he was somewhere deep in his own head.

I waved my hand in front of Wyatt's face. "You figure anything out since this morning?"

"No," he said, shaking his head. "I still don't know who the leaders of the ninja clans are."

Glancing at the front offices, I said, "We could always go to the principal with this. Tell him that a bunch of ninjas are training on the roof aaaaand… I'm just now realizing how crazy it all sounds when I say it out loud."

"Right?" Brayden said. "*We'll* be the ones locked away in detention."

"Doesn't matter," Naomi said. "Those ninjas aren't on the roof anymore. They prob'ly cleared out right after we got away."

"Could we challenge them?" I suggested.

114

Wyatt sat up. "I thought you didn't fight."

"No, not to a fight," I said. "To, like, a dance off or – geez, nevermind. I knew that answer was dumb before I finished the sentence. What's wrong with me today?"

"How about we do nothing?" Naomi said.

"I *like* that idea!" I said.

"Seriously though," she said. "For all we know, those ninjas could just be a buncha kids that want to hang out and practice ninja moves. Maybe there *isn't* some kind of ultimate plan they're working on. What if all this running around and chasing they're doing is *because* you guys keep messing with them?"

Naomi totally had a point. The only times I ran into them that week was because *I* was the one going after them.

The first time was on Monday when I helped Wyatt.

The second time was when I used myself as bait.

And the third time was earlier that morning when we barged in on them drinking coffee.

All three times, it was *me* going to them.

"I think we should leave them alone," Naomi said. "I bet this is just some kind of lame-o club for them. If that's all it is, then we're fine."

"But *I'm* not fine," Wyatt said. "It's *my* lame-o club to lead! Not *theirs!*"

Naomi looked right at Wyatt. "Bummer, man."

Wyatt's jaw flexed, but he didn't say anything. He stood up, and then he walked away down the hall. Olivia ran to catch up with him.

Wyatt definitely wasn't happy. What did he think was going to happen though? That he was going to get his red ninjas back just like that? There *had* to be a part of him that knew it might not happen, right?

## Thursday. 3:00 PM. After school.

Everyone on the team was in the science lab after school. Everyone except Wyatt. He didn't show up, but it was possible he was running late.

Slug and Brayden had finished the shell they were working on and were letting the paint dry before putting it over Hup-Hup, our robot.

Zoe and Faith kept switching Hup-Hup on and off, amazed that the machine was working perfectly. It *was* kind of cute how it just kept waving.

Carlyle's team was quiet for a change. Wanna know why? Because they weren't even in there.

I peeked over the cloth partition to get a glimpse of their robot. I was shocked to see that all the pieces from Tenderfoot Industries were still spread out on the floor in messy piles. I wasn't sure Carlyle's team even *had* a robot.

Dante was in his corner. He was sitting on a chair, gawking at the broken robot that he trashed the day before. "How could I have done this…" he whispered to himself.

That kid had problems.

"That's the face of a kid who can't even anymore," Naomi said when she saw me staring at Dante.

"Can't even what?" I said.

"You know," Naomi said. "He is *unable* to even. He's *lost* the ability to even. *He can't even!*"

"Someday I'm gonna make a poster that says 'you *can* even,'" I said.

"Where's Wyatt?" Zoe asked, finally realizing the seventh member of our team was absent.

"Prob'ly blowing off steam somewhere," I said. "Punching tree trunks or something."

Faith raised her eyebrows. "Is he mad?"

"He's not happy," I said.

"What happened?" Zoe asked, concerned. "Did you guys get in a fight? I *knew* he was trouble!"

"No," I said. "Nothing like that. He's going through some things. I bet he just needed to be alone."

"I did," Wyatt's voice came from the door. He was leaning against the frame with his hands in his pockets. "I'm better now though."

"Oh, good," Zoe said. "You're a member of our team, and I'd hate for you to miss out on anything."

"Where's Olivia?" Brayden asked.

"She had to take off or something," Wyatt said. "Her dad was going to pick her up today. Nevermind her though. I wanted... to... um..."

Everyone fell silent as Wyatt stumbled over words like they were speed bumps.

"I know that I... it's not been the greatest... um..." he stopped, taking a deep breath. Finally, he said, "I'm sorry I was kind of a wad today."

Whoa. Was Wyatt apologizing to me? He was looking right at me. There was the word "sorry" in his sentence that *wasn't* followed with a "but..."

Yup. I think Wyatt was apologizing. It was slow and awkward, like nails on a chalkboard. I just wanted it to be over already!

"It's cool," I said, nodding.

"How were you a wad today?" Zoe asked, confused. She wasn't with us when Wyatt stormed off at lunch.

"I don't really wanna talk about it anymore," Wyatt said. "Chase was right. He's been right the whole time. And I'm just saying sorry."

I think Faith's mind was blown because her jaw was

dropped and her eyes were wide.

"Y'know," Zoe said, "When Chase let you on the team, I wasn't happy about it. I don't think any of us were. We all thought you were gonna be a jerk, but you proved us wrong. Especially with all the snacks."

Wyatt's eyes softened. "Good! Then I guess it was a good thing I ordered some cupcakes for our final day working as a team."

"There's a lot more happening at Buchanan this year," Zoe said. "Maybe we'll all be on the same team again."

"That'd be awesome," Wyatt said, glancing at his watch. "Oh, the cupcakes'll be here any second."

"It's time for our break anyways," Zoe said, standing from her chair. "Are they delivering them to the lobby?"

Wyatt nodded.

"Cool," Zoe said. "Faith and I will go grab them. Anyone else wanna come too?"

Brayden stood, smiling. "Totes. We'll have to wait outside for them though because the doors are locked after school lets out. Someone will have to let us back in, so one of us has to stay in the lobby."

"That's fine," Zoe said. "I could use some fresh air. Some fresh *cold* air."

"I'll stay in the lobby," I said. I didn't feel like standing outside in the cold.

"Me too," Wyatt said.

After that, we all made our way downstairs to the lobby.

About a minute later, Wyatt and I were sitting on the top step in the nook, watching through the window as the rest of our team jumped off the benches outside.

Naomi wasn't with them though. She said she forgot something at her locker, and went that way instead.

Wyatt and I didn't say anything to each other. I wasn't sure if it was because he was angry, or embarrassed.

Without warning, Wyatt jumped to his feet, staring down the hall.

I didn't have to ask what he saw because I knew the look on his face. It was the same look I had whenever I saw the same thing.

There were ninjas in the hallway, and they were coming for us.

**Thursday, 3:10 PM. The hallways.**

I looked out the window. The cupcakes Wyatt ordered hadn't been delivered yet, so the rest of Team Cooper would be outside for another few minutes. That was good. It meant they weren't in danger when the holiday ninjas stormed the halls.

The front office was empty. Principal Davis was nowhere to be seen. And then I realized that it wasn't the teachers who were gone at the worst times. It was that the ninjas waited *until* they was gone.

Wyatt walked toward the middle of the lobby. "I can hear their footsteps," he said.

"That means they *want* you to hear their footsteps," I said.

"If *I* was still their leader, then it would mean that," Wyatt said, "but since I'm *not* their leader, it probably just means they're terrible ninjas."

Pulling my mask over my face, I said, "You should probably get your mask out."

"I don't *have* a mask," Wyatt growled. "Remember? They *took* it from me."

"You don't have extras?"

119

"Uh, yeah, I had a *hundred* extras," Wyatt said. "I gave them to the kids in my ninja clan before I got canned!"

The footsteps were quickly getting louder, but they weren't just coming from the one hallway. They were also coming from the hallway on the other side of the lobby.

"They're gonna corner us out here," Wyatt said.

"There's no way they'd try to fight us, right?" I asked, unsure. "I mean, we're two guys against their what? Hundred ninjas?"

"It's probably not that many," Wyatt said. "Trust me, I know. Trying to get that many ninjas to work together on *one* thing is impossible."

"Okay, so *less* than a hundred, but more than two," I said. "Ugh... sounds like a story problem." I paused, and then chuckled. "One ninja clan leaves their dojo travelling at 10 miles per hour. A second ninja clans leaves *their* dojo going 15 miles per hour. How long will it take for the second ninja clan to pass the first one?"

Wyatt sighed, watching the hallway. "You got the two ninja clans leaving two *different* dojos. It doesn't work. What if the dojos were on opposite ends of the planet? Then the second ninja clan would *never* pass the first one."

"I, uh..." I said, racking my brain trying to remember what I even asked. "Um, nevermind. It was just a joke."

"Get your head back in the game, Cooper," Wyatt said. "We gotta act fast. Those ninjas are gonna turn the corner any second!"

"We can't go outside," I said. "And both hallways are out, so..."

"It's too late!" Wyatt said, pointing at a group of kids running straight toward the lobby.

I spun around to check the hall behind me. Kids had already turned the corner there too. My heart was about to drop until I realized the students weren't wearing ninja outfits. They were wearing gym clothes.

Tearing my mask off my head, I stuffed it back into my hood before anyone could see me wearing it.

Relieved, I watched as the two groups of kids ran past each other in the lobby. It was the track team. Sometimes they ran laps in the hallways when it was too cold to run outside.

"Comin' through, guys!" the track team captain said as he ran by.

Wyatt swallowed hard and then let out a sigh. He looked at me as the track team passed us on both sides. The crowd was thick enough that it was hard to see the walls behind them.

"Maybe we *are* a little paranoid," Wyatt said to me.

The track team started to thin out, and I was able to see the walls between each passing student. After another couple seconds, the track team was gone. Wyatt and I watched as they disappeared down the hallway.

"That was a little freaky," I said.

And then a girl's voice spoke from behind Wyatt and me. "Not as freaky as us," she said.

I almost jumped out of my skin when I spun around. I could tell Wyatt was surprised too, because he stumbled back when he turned.

There, facing the two of us, was a small pack of green ninjas.

Wyatt and I turned around to run, but the ninjas were too quick. They had already circled around us, keeping us from going anyway. The only spot they left open was the door to the cafeteria.

I went straight for the lunchroom because I wasn't about to stay in the middle of a ninja mosh pit. Wyatt followed me, pushing me through the door once I pressed the handle down.

# UGH... THEY'RE EVEN POSING.

For the second time that week, Wyatt and I fell through a door together.

We rolled to a stop on the cold floor of the cafeteria. Lunch tables had been folded in half and set up in a long line down the back of the lunchroom. The huge fluorescent lamps on the ceiling had been switched off.

The sun was still out, but it was dark in the cafeteria since the windows were all tinted. It looked like it was the middle of the night.

"Get off me," Wyatt groaned.

"Sorry," I said, getting to my feet.

The green ninjas stepped through the door calmly. They knew Wyatt and I had nowhere to run, so they weren't in any hurry.

And then a single red ninja appeared behind them. He was wearing a yellow cape over one shoulder. I had seen him once before, but not for more than a couple seconds.

"What do you want?" Wyatt said. "Not enough that you guys took my mask, huh?"

"*I* didn't take your mask," the girl ninja said. The rest of the green ninjas stood behind her with their arms folded. She must've been their new leader.

The red ninja in the back said nothing. His yellow caped was draped across his shoulder.

"Then what?" Wyatt said loudly, but not shouting.

"We're here to deliver a message," she said.

"And what's that?" Wyatt asked, clenching his fists.

The ninja took a moment to answer, eyeballing Wyatt. "Give up," she finally said. "We *know* you've been looking for us all week. Stop it now, or else."

"Or else?" I repeated, kind of surprised. "A threat? Really?"

The ninja's eyes darted at me, but she didn't answer.

"I'm not giving up until I get my ninja clan back!" Wyatt said, pointing at the red ninja in the back. "You messed with the wrong kid, pal!"

"What makes you think you'll get it back?" the green ninja leader asked. "Your ninjas have *abandoned* you."

"Then I won't stop until *every* ninja clan here is *destroyed*," Wyatt said.

The green ninjas didn't like that.

As a group, the green ninjas stomped across the cafeteria with eyes on fire. I'm sure their faces were angry too, but all I could see were their crazy eyes.

The red ninja continued to stand perfectly still, like he was only there to watch the action.

Wyatt dashed forward to meet the green ninjas head on.

The whole thing had gotten out of hand. The doors to the cafeteria were too far from me to try and escape. Wyatt and I were about to get our butts handed to us on a silver platter, and why? Because I had to stick my nose where it didn't belong! I had nothing to do with Wyatt and his red ninja clan! I shouldn't have even been there!

At that moment, a door slammed open so hard that it shook the floor of the lunchroom. The green ninjas stopped in place. So did Wyatt.

I *might've* yelped like a frightened baby deer. I don't know. There was so much happening that it was hard to tell. Maybe there *was* a frightened baby deer somewhere in the cafeteria. How could someone even know there *wasn't*? Here – *prove* to me that there *wasn't* a frightened baby deer in there. See? You can't.

The lunchroom was dark enough that all I could make

out were the shadows of other ninjas pouring out of the door that had opened at the back of the room. There were dozens of them. Literally, dozens!

And they were all wearing black. The same color my ninja clan wore. Chalk dust poured from the door, masking them slightly. They looked like floating ninja ghosts.

"What the heck?" the green ninja leader whispered.

The black ninjas stopped right outside the door they came out of. They stood like statues and said nothing, which was scarier looking than it sounded.

The green ninja leader stepped backward as her ninjas did the same. She didn't say anything.

I squinted at the black ninjas, trying to see who they were because I didn't have a clue. My ninja clan only had five members in it – Brayden, Gidget, Slug, Naomi, and me.

So who were all the ninjas at the back of the cafeteria?

And then I saw her. It was just a glimpse, but I instantly knew what was happening. Naomi was hiding in the door where all the ninjas had come from. She was the only other member of the team that didn't go outside. She winked at me when we made eye contact.

She made good on her promise. She was my secret guardian ninja. She probably didn't even need to get anything from her locker. She only said that to keep an eye out for me.

Earlier that week, I told her about how some black balloons saved me from getting my butt kicked. Naomi told me the stage was full of black balloons.

When I squinted, I could see that the heads of the ninjas were the balloons I had told her about. She had painted eyes on them. Their bodies looked like black crinkled up garbage bags.

Naomi had made an army of fake ninjas.

The green ninjas didn't notice because they backed out of the cafeteria too quickly. Even the single red ninja was worried about being outnumbered.

Puffs of chalk dust burst around the ninjas, and they began to disappear one by one. Not, like, magically because I could see them run away after throwing their little chalk pouch on the floor. Ninja vanish? More like ninja hobble away.

The two holiday ninja leaders were the last in the cafeteria. They were still staring across the room at the fake army.

And then the worst possible thing that could happen, happened.

One of the black balloons popped.

The green ninja shrieked. "*His head exploded! His head just*—wait a second..."

The balloons were a couple days old. Of course they had become weak. It wouldn't have taken much to pop one of them.

The green ninja turned around to command her other ninjas to attack again, but they were gone. The red ninja grabbed her elbow when she tried to run back to us.

"No!" the red ninja growled. "There's no time for this! They won't listen so we'll *make* them pay!"

"That's such a *bad guy* thing to say!" I said.

"Have fun explaining to the rest of *Team Cooper* how *Hup-Hup* was crushed," the red ninja said.

"*Hup-Hup?*" I asked. My heart sunk when I realized he was talking about the robot Team Cooper had built. "You *wouldn't*..."

But the two leaders of the holiday ninjas were already out the door and sprinting toward the stairs.

### Thursday. 3:20 PM. The science lab.

Wyatt and I ran as fast as we could to stop the two ninjas headed for the science lab, but they were too fast. They skipped, like, four steps at a time on the stairs!

The rest of my team was still outside waiting for the cupcake delivery. I was actually bummed that they were out there because if they were inside, I knew they would've kept Hup-Hup safe.

At the moment though, the robot was alone in the room and unguarded.

When we got to the top of the stairs, the two ninjas had just turned the corner.

"We're not gonna catch them in time!" Wyatt said.

"We can't just stop though!" I said, feeling my side cramp up.

I was running so fast that I couldn't turn the corner without slamming into the wall. The pain that shot through my body made me freeze for a second.

The science lab was only a few doors down, and it was open. The two ninjas were already inside.

Wyatt passed me, slowing down as he got to the door. I pushed through the pain and caught up with him.

We were just in time… to watch the red ninja dropkick our robot, sending parts flying in all directions.

I dropped to my knees. "*Noooooooooo!*"

"*You're just a poser!*" Wyatt shouted. He was just as upset about our robot as I was. "Just some *kid* that's pretending to be the leader of my ninja clan! If you're gonna steal my clan out from under me, then at least do it without wearing your mask! Show me your face, you coward!"

The red ninja stood up straight, and then he did exactly as Wyatt asked. He took off his mask.

Wyatt's knees almost gave out from under him, but he managed to keep himself up. I choked as I caught my breath on the floor. The new leader of the red ninjas was staring Wyatt right in the eyes.

It was Carlyle. The pirate. Wyatt's cousin.

CARLYLE
...THE PIRATE.

...ew.

NOT SURE HOW HIS CAPE IS BLOWING IN THE WIND.

Carlyle's yellow cape swooped out, and I saw that it wasn't *just* a cape. It was a pirate flag with a picture of a skull.

Wyatt's face grew red with anger. He was stunned, but not shocked like I was. "Figures it was you," he said calmly.

127

"Can't get any kids into your little pirate club, so you just take *my* ninja clan instead. Weak, dude. Weak."

"Ye lost control of yer crew long ago, mate!" Carlyle said.

"Why are you still talking like that?" I said as I got to my feet. "Are you a pirate or a ninja?"

"I be a *ninja pirate*, ya pox-faced kraken!" Carlyle said, squeezing one eye shut.

"That's not even a thing!" I said.

I *hate* to admit it, but... a ninja pirate *did* kind of sound cool. Can you imagine? Sailing the seas in a pirate boat, and then taking to land as a ninja? Hey, it wasn't *pirates* I hated. It was when kids *talked* like pirates. *That's* what I hated.

"It is now, ye parrot lovin' sea bass," Carlyle said.

I put my hands up. "Uh, alright. Enough with the pirate insults. It's a little over the top."

Wyatt stepped forward. "I didn't lose control of *anything*, you backstabber. You *took* my ninjas from me! And then you made them steal my mask!"

"Aye," Carlyle said. "You were lame as a leader, cousin. There was so much more ye coulda done with your ninjas, but ye never did."

"Like sell a bunch of t-shirts and garbage?" Wyatt said.

Carlyle laughed. "Do ye really think this has got t'do with merchandise, cousin?"

In that moment of awkward silence, my brain connected all the dots. "You're jealous," I said to Carlyle. "That's what this is, isn't it? Wyatt's ninja clan is bigger than your pirate crew, and now you're taking what he's built."

"Keep yer mouth shut," Carlyle said.

"You snuck your way into my ninja clan," Wyatt said, connecting the same dots I had. "And staged a mutiny against me..."

"You're only now realizing that?" Carlyle said.

"Yes!" Wyatt shouted.

I watched the two cousins shout it out at each other. I don't believe Wyatt had a clue that Carlyle was the kid who took his ninja clan, but I also don't believe he was surprised.

The pirates at Buchanan School had grown weak. Instead of building them back up, Carlyle just took red ninjas from his cousin. Wyatt was bound to find out sooner or later, and being Wyatt, he wasn't going to take it well.

The whole thing had gone from being a simple ninja clan takeover to something *much* bigger…

It was a battle between two families.

And somehow I had gotten stuck in the middle of it.

Whoops.

And then believe it or not, things got even *more* twisted up…

Carlyle nodded. "Yer at yer wits end, cousin. Give yerself up, and I'll keep ya from walkin' the plank."

"Walk *what* plank?" Wyatt huffed. "You're *such* a poser that I'm not even surprised it was you that staged this whole thing!"

"No?" Carlyle said. "Then how's this for a surprise?"

The green ninja leader untied their mask, and pulled it off their head.

It was Olivia.

OLIVIA!

LEADER OF THE GREEN NINJAS!

Wyatt actually *was* shocked that time. His bottom lip quivered. "…babe?"

129

"I was gonna break up with ya," Olivia said. "But then ya went and got yourself on Chase's team."

"Made it too easy to spy on yer robot," Carlyle said.

At that moment, Team Cooper stepped through the doors behind us. They stopped in place, staring at the bizarre scene that was in front of them. Naomi was the only one from the team who wasn't there.

I couldn't even imagine how it looked to Zoe. There we were, Wyatt and I, standing over our destroyed robot. Carlyle and Olivia wearing ninja costumes, but without their masks.

A cloud of chalk dust burst around Carlyle and Olivia, and then they were gone. I actually had no idea how they left the room because the only way out was through the door that Team Cooper was standing in.

Zoe stared at the pieces of the robot we all worked so hard to build.

The rest of my friends looked like life had just slapped them across the face. They were sad and defeated.

Zoe glared at me. *"What did you do?"* she growled through her teeth.

"I didn't do any of this!" I said defensively. "You saw who did it!"

"No!" Zoe shouted. "This is all because of you and your

little ninja game! You *killed* our project with this stupid secret you have! It never bothered me before, but it never affected anything I did before! You've gone too far this time!"

Zoe didn't know how many times my ninja lifestyle had actually affected her. I kept trouble from finding her *many* times before, but she didn't know that. And I preferred to keep it that way.

"But I—" I starting saying.

"*Neh!*" Zoe snipped. It was her way of making me keep my mouth shut. "I know what I saw in here. I saw you and Wyatt and Carlyle and Olivia, but you know what? I don't blame them! I blame *you!* If you didn't run around the school pretending to be a ninja, then we'd still have a shot at winning tomorrow! You *know* how important this was to me! You *know* Dr. Tenderfoot was a big deal to me!"

I tried to talk again, but Zoe shut me down with another "*Neh!*"

"You vouched for Wyatt!" Zoe said.

Everyone behind her was upset with me too because they nodded, agreeing with my cousin.

"And Wyatt vouched for Olivia!" Zoe said. "Okay, so Olivia and Carlyle are working together? Too bad she was hanging out on *our* side of the room all week!"

"She was a spy," I said under my breath.

"What normal kid can say that seriously?" Zoe said. "I know I can't! I can't go around talking about ninjas and pirates and spies without sounding like a nutcase!"

Zoe stopped. Her chest was heaving up and down like she was going to have a panic attack.

"And *you*," she said, looking at Wyatt. "Of course Carlyle did this! Of course Olivia did this! Of course you're the one behind it all! I guess we're all just paying the price for trusting someone we *shouldn't* have trusted!"

Wyatt started to talk, but the rest of the team chimed in, not letting him get a word out.

"Dude," Slug said. "Was this your plan the whole time?"

"Yeah," Faith said. "Were you playing us?"

"Of course he was! It's so obvi!" Brayden said.

Wyatt didn't bother saying anything else. He pushed his way through the team and walked out the door.

And then the rest of my team left the room, one after the other, in total silence, until I was all alone.

Everything happened so fast, that I was still in shock. Leaning my back against the wall, I slid down until I was sitting on the floor. In just twenty short minutes, everything had gone from absolutely great to absolutely awful.

The broken parts of Hup-Hup were spread across the floor in front of me.

I'd made mistakes and messed things up in the past, but this time felt different. Like, somehow it felt worse.

Much, much worse.

### Thursday. 3:35 PM. The school parking lot.

I was in a funk. I could barely even bring myself to clean up the mess that Carlyle made when he booted Hup-Hup across the room. There were tiny pieces everywhere that I scooped into a small pile, but that was as far as I got when Zoe texted me.

My phone buzzed in my front pocket. When I pulled it out, I unlocked the screen and read the message from my cousin.

*"my dads gonna be here any minute"*

It was short and had no punctuation, and since it was a text message, I read it like she was angry. Texts are weird like that. If someone just texts *"OK,"* then I'll think they were mad at me. But if they text *"OK!,"* then I'll know they *weren't* mad.

The mess was still on the floor, but I was beat. It would mean getting to school early again, but cleaning could wait until the morning.

I grabbed my book bag, pulled one of the straps over my shoulder, and headed down to the lobby.

The rest of Team Cooper was already gone. Zoe was alone on a bench outside, staring at nothing. She was slouching, which was unlike her. She always nagged at me about my poor posture.

The air felt colder than normal. It bit at my cheeks the second I stepped outside.

I didn't say anything when I sat next to her.

She sighed. But not the kind of sigh that was like, "*look at me,*" but the kind of sigh that said she was sad.

"Zoe," I finally said. "I'm *really* sorry."

She took a deep breath, still staring at nothing. "I know," she said.

"No," I said. "I mean, I'm really, *really* sorry."

Zoe looked at me. "I know you are," she said. "But it's just a robot. There are worse things happening in the world. Zoe Cooper getting her project destroyed is small time."

"But it was a big deal to you," I said. "I know that I let you down with, y'know… my *ninja* stuff."

"Why do you still do it?" Zoe asked. "Why do you still play that game with them?"

Zoe knew it was more than a game to me.

"If you didn't do any of that," Zoe continued, "you wouldn't have any problems."

"I don't know why I do it," I said, but the truth was I knew exactly why.

There were a lot of bad eggs at Buchanan, and if there wasn't something there to keep them in check, the balance would shift in their favor. *I* was that "something."

But I couldn't tell Zoe any of that.

"I know I shouldn't have trusted Wyatt," I said.

Zoe tilted her head back and groaned like she was about to say something she didn't want to. "I can't believe I'm about to say this but… while I was waiting for my dad out here, I saw Wyatt leave through one of the side doors. He didn't look happy, like, at all. His face kept twitching. It looked like he was really beating himself up about Hup-Hup."

"Really…" I said.

Zoe nodded. "Mm-hmm. If he was in on it, then why wasn't he with Carlyle or Olivia? He had the look of a boy who had been burned by his best friends. I really don't think Wyatt is to blame this time."

I was mad at Wyatt, but I felt the same way that Zoe did.

Yes, he's one of the bad eggs Buchanan. Yes, he's been a rusty nail stuck in my big toe since the first week of school. And yes, his plans were always cranked to eleven on the evil-villain scale.

But Wyatt wasn't the one who destroyed our robot. That was Carlyle along with Olivia's help.

If I really wanted to be fair to Wyatt, then I had to admit he was *probably* innocent, no matter how he had acted in the past.

Zoe's dad pulled his car into the parking lot.

"I'll figure out how to make this right," I said.

Zoe smiled softly. "I know you will," she said. "You always do."

With less than a day until the competition, I had no idea how I could fix any of the mess I had created.

At that point, my life sounded like it'd be a lot easier if I just gave up and let Carlyle's team win by default.

**Friday. 7:10 AM. The science lab.**

I was walking down the hallway on the second floor, heading for the science lab when I noticed that the door was propped open. Someone had gotten there before me, which wasn't a big surprise since it *was* the day of the robot competition.

What *was* surprising was that it was Wyatt.

He sat on a backwards chair the way he always did. On the floor in front of him were the shattered parts of our robot, spread out in such a way that it looked like he was trying to figure out how to put it back together.

When he saw me, he nodded once.

"What're you doing?" I asked.

"What's it look like?" Wyatt said.

"It looks like you're trying to fix the robot."

"Then *that's* what I'm doing."

I didn't know what to say. Should I have brought up Carlyle? Olivia? It's not like Wyatt *wasn't* there when they totally stabbed him in the back. But was it something that even needed to be talked about?

The fact that he was even there had to mean *something*, right?

136

"What do you think?" I asked, taking the seat next to his. "Is Hup-Hup done for?"

Wyatt shrugged his shoulders. "I wouldn't even know where to start. I had to set it out like this so I could see what it's *supposed* to look like. But all I see are random parts."

"Let's just sweep it into the trash then," I said. "We'll clean it up and throw in the towel."

"No!" Wyatt said angrily. "I will *not* let Carlyle steamroll right through me."

"I think he already did," I said.

"Dude," Wyatt said, sitting up. "I'm not gonna roll over and die like that. Carlyle, my own *cousin*, burned me. Olivia, my *girlfriend*, burned me. *All* my ninjas… *burned* me. I got no one anymore, but I'm *not* defeated. I *hate* defeat. *That's* what I'm doing here. I'm not giving up."

I thought it was ironic that Wyatt was in the same place that I had found myself in many times before. It's not a fun place.

The way Wyatt set Hup-Hup out on the floor made it really easy for me to figure out how to put the machine back together.

I sat on my knees and started putting the pieces back in their place. Wyatt helped when he could, but it was mostly pointing at parts and asking if I needed them.

Even though Carlyle had kicked our robot, the damage actually wasn't as bad as I thought. Most of the parts clicked back into their spot. Sure, the thing might've been an ugly version of what it used to be, but at least it wasn't a shattered mess of broken dreams anymore.

Once it was finished, Wyatt and I looked back and forth between the robot and the *many* extra parts we had leftover.

"So those things were in the first version of the robot?" Wyatt asked.

"Yeah," I said. "But not the second version. Hope they weren't important."

"Guess we'll find out," Wyatt said.

Pushing all the spare parts aside, I reached my fingers under the robot and flipped the switch to turn it on.

But Hup-Hup didn't move. Something buzzed quietly from the robot, but none of the parts were doing anything. The light bulb on top didn't even flicker.

"C'mon, man," I said, flipping the switch back and

forth.

"Maybe those extra parts *were* important," Wyatt said, glancing at the pile of junk we had swept up.

"What'd you do that first day it didn't work?" I asked, looking at the battery pack.

"Oh, the battery wasn't fully connecting," Wyatt said. "I just made sure it connected. Push the battery down hard. If that's the problem again, it should fix it."

I took Wyatt's advice and smashed my thumb against the battery. At the same time, I tried switching it on again, but nothing happened except for the quiet buzz.

Studying the guts of the robot, I followed the wires from the battery pack to the small motor at the shoulder, and then studied the gears to see if something was just stuck.

Finally, after a couple of minutes, I admitted, "I have no idea what I'm looking at."

"Step aside, rookie," Wyatt said, staring at the machine for a moment before he said, "Yeah, I got nothing."

And then a voice came from behind one of the hanging sheets that separated the room. "The problem's probably with your wires."

Wyatt and I looked at each other, surprised that anyone else was in the room.

"Uh, hello?" I said.

"Hi," the voice replied.

"So, um, how long have you been there?"

"The whole time."

"You didn't hear anything that we—" I started saying, but the voice cut me off.

"I heard every word you said. Carlyle, Olivia, ninjas, and all."

"Darn it," Wyatt mouthed. "It's Dante."

Dante peeked out from behind his sheet. "But I don't care about any of that."

Wyatt and I weren't sure what to say, so we said nothing.

But Dante meant it when he said he didn't care because he quickly changed the subject, pointing at Hup-Hup. "If it's not your battery pack, then it's probably your wires. I heard it making some noises, so it's *trying* to work."

"Ummmm," I said, pinching the plastic coated wires between my fingers. They *did* feel loose, but I really didn't know how they were supposed to feel.

Dante could tell. "Look at the part where the wires hook into the gearbox at the top," he said. "What's it look like?"

Following the wires with my fingers, I found the spot Dante was talking about. The plastic on each of the wires was peeled back, probably from when Carlyle booted it. The thin copper wires underneath were shredded, barely making contact with the gearbox.

"They're about to fall off," I said loudly enough so Dante could hear it, but he was already hovering over my shoulder.

"See that?" Dante said, pointing at the frayed end of the wires. "The robot's buzzing because it's working, but not getting enough power since that connection is busted. All ya gotta do is..." Dante trailed off as he pinched the frayed wires. He rolled his fingers back and forth to get the wires to stay in place. "Try it now."

I flipped the switch. Hup-Hup jumped to life, raising his arm while his hand spun in circles. The light from the bulb was so bright it almost blinded me.

"Nice!" I said, excited.

It was ugly and sloppily put back together, but our robot was working again.

"Thanks, dude," I said, looking back at his side of the room. "You know what you're doing with this stuff, so… what happened over there with *your* robot?"

Dante pressed his lips to the side. "Robotics is kind of a hobby for me. I love working on junk like this, but… I get frustrated when things don't work. I mean, I was already frustrated 'cause nobody wanted to be on my team, but y'know, whatever I guess."

I felt bad for the kid as he walked back to his corner of the science lab.

"There are a ton of things these robots can do," Dante said. "I think I was trying to fit too many of those things into one package. It was too much."

"Bummer," Wyatt said in a way that sounded like he didn't care.

"No bigs," Dante said. "Good luck with your robot. You only have Carlyle to worry about. I completely trashed my robot so I'm out."

Hup-Hup kept waving his little arm up and down, like he was saying goodbye to Dante. Wyatt had a stupid grin on his face as he watched our robot do the one trick it was created to do.

The hairs on my arm stood on end. Dante helped fix our robot, which meant we *didn't* have to sit back and let Carlyle win. There was still a chance. School didn't start for another twenty minutes. With that much time, I could grab some breakfast in the cafeteria, or… I could keep working on Hup-Hup.

"Dante!" I said before he sunk back into his corner of the room.

He spun around. "Hmm?"

"What *else* would you do to this thing?" I asked.

Dante smiled as he walked back to Team Cooper's corner of the room, going on and on about all the little things we could add to the gears to make the robot do even more with very little changes.

While Dante was talking, Wyatt leaned closer to me. He knew exactly what I was thinking.

"We *have* our team," Wyatt whispered.

I looked Wyatt in the eye. "Be like water, bro."

The muscles in Wyatt's jaw twitched. He wasn't happy with it, but he didn't have a choice. I was the team leader. Not him.

And Dante was now part of my team.

**Friday. 8:00 AM. The library.**

Dante and I carried our robot down the stairs carefully.
We had covered it with one of the bed sheets so nobody could
see it before the competition.

Wyatt went to the library to make sure we had a spot up
front, like we even needed it though. We were *in* the
competition – of course we'd have a spot up front. They
probably even set a "reserved" sign on our desk.

Wyatt just didn't feel like helping. He wasn't happy that
Dante was part of the team, but I didn't care. Dante had been
having problems all week, and I don't even know why it took
me *that* long to come up with the idea for him to join Team
Cooper. All this junk about the red and green ninjas had been
more of a distraction than I thought.

Carlyle and his team never showed up to the science lab,
but I snuck a peek at their section of the room. It had been
completely cleaned out as if they were never there. Obviously
they were, but it meant they had come and gotten their stuff
already.

Their robot was probably gonna blow ours away. I knew
it, especially after Carlyle destroyed ours. But staying in the
competition wasn't about winning anymore. It was about

142

showing Carlyle that we weren't going to sit back and let him do what he wanted.

But even as Dante and I carried Hup-Hup down the hall, I had a glimmer of hope in the back of my mind that *maybe* we had a chance at winning.

I sent a text to my friends before going to the library, letting them know that I had a surprise, and that I hoped they showed up.

Principal Davis held the library door open so Dante and I could carry our robot through.

Kids parted ways as we walked through the huge room. School had started, but the competition hadn't yet, so everyone was just hanging out until something happened. The library was just as packed as it had been on Monday. Dr. Tenderfoot wasn't anywhere I could see.

When we got to our spot in front of the staircase at the center of the room, I thought we'd have a table to set Hup-Hup down on, but we didn't. Instead, the middle of the room was taped off and kept empty. It almost looked like a boxing ring.

Carlyle's team was in one corner. They were huddled around their robot, which was also covered with a sheet. Carlyle was in the middle of the huddle, but Olivia wasn't with him.

Wyatt was waiting in the opposite corner all by himself. Zoe and the rest of the team weren't there. Without my cousin and my team, my brain felt foggy, like I was just watching my life from behind a dirty window.

"About time," Wyatt said. "What took you so long?"

"What took us so long was that there were only two of us carrying this beast," I said. "We woulda been here sooner if you helped."

"You coulda just asked," Wyatt said.

"I *did!*" I said.

Wyatt pushed his hands into his front pockets. "Didn't hear ya."

"Right," I said.

Dante and I carefully set our robot on the floor, and then pushed it gently until it was in the ring.

I looked over my shoulder, hoping to see the rest of my team, but they weren't there. I checked my phone for texts, but I didn't have any.

"Have you seen the others yet?" I asked Wyatt.

143

He shook his head. "Nope," he said. "But I sent them a text about how they didn't need to show up."

"*You did what?*" I said. "Dude, what's the matter with you?"

"What?" Wyatt said. "They don't need to be here! They didn't help fix our robot, did they? It was just you and me in that room!"

"And me," Dante added.

Wyatt ignored Dante. "Why should they be the ones standing with us when *we* were the ones who did all the work?"

I couldn't believe what I was hearing. Was Wyatt delusional?

"Because we *didn't* do all the work," I said. "We *all* worked on it, and then because of *you*, it was destroyed!"

"And then you and I fixed it," Wyatt said, nodding at me like we were on the same page.

"And me," Dante added.

Again, Wyatt ignored him. "Dude, what's the big deal? That means this bombastic prize will be just for us. What d'you think it'll be? A million bucks? How sweet would that be?"

"I don't want that!" I said.

Wyatt looked at me like I was crazy. "You... *don't* want a million bucks?"

"No, of course I want a million bucks," I said. "But I don't want to shut out the rest of the team!"

"Chase, listen," Wyatt said. "You're not thinking of the bigger picture. Think of yourself for once, dude. Your chums will be mad, but they'll get over it."

"Not the point," Zoe's voice said from behind us.

Everyone from the team was right next to her. All five of them – Brayden, Faith, Gidget, Slug, and Naomi. And they looked angry.

"Cripes," Wyatt said. "I told you guys you didn't need to be here!"

Zoe laughed loudly. "Where do you think we were gonna go?" she asked. "This is a school wide event! Plus I'm the *president* of the sixth grade class who *planned* it!"

"Did you think we'd just stay home or something?" Faith asked, nudging her way past Wyatt. She lifted a piece of the sheet covering our robot. "Is this Hup-Hup? Did you really fix him?"

"Uh, yeah," Wyatt said. "*Chase* and *I* fixed him."

"With my help," Dante added sheepishly.

Wyatt tried to ignore him again by talking, but I shut him down right away.

"Oh, and also, Dante's on our team now," I said. "He was the one who helped us fix it. Without him, Hup-Hup would still be dead. Just a dead cow machine."

I think it was because of the way Wyatt felt about Dante that I was worried what the others would think. I expected a little bit of conflict, but it never came.

The rest of my team shrugged it off and didn't even care.

"Cool," Slug said, putting his hand on Dante's shoulder. "But if you're on our team, then you're gonna have to work on your anger management, okay?"

Dante LOL'd.

"Nobody cares?" Wyatt asked.

Everyone shook their heads. It was kind of funny. Wyatt had such a problem with letting another person on the team, but it didn't bother anyone else.

The lights in the library switched off and then back on again, letting everyone know the competition was going to start in a minute.

"Have you seen Dr. Tenderfoot yet?" Zoe asked, looking over everyone's head.

"No," I said. "He's supposed to be here, right?"

"I think he was here before school," Zoe said. "But I never got a chance to see him."

"Maybe his helicopter hasn't dropped him off in the parking lot yet," Brayden said.

"He came by helicopter?" Naomi said. "Man, how cool is that?"

"Super cool," Dr. Tenderfoot said, walking past us toward the staircase. "But definitely *too* cool for this cool guy. I still drive myself to the places I need to go."

Dr. Tenderfoot was wearing the exact same thing as he did on Monday. He had his top hat, tuxedo jacket, jeans, and sneakers on. A small chain dangled from the monocle on his right eye.

Tenderfoot took to the staircase and grabbed the microphone. "Welcome, welcome, children of Buchanan School! It's been entirely too long since we last met, and I

145

hope life has been good to you since."

A couple kids clapped, but stopped when they realized nobody else was.

Brayden sprayed a shot of cologne on his chest. "What?" he said at everyone staring at him. "In case we win! I wanna smell good for the ladies!"

"As you know, we have three teams that will be participating in the competition," Tenderfoot continued. He pulled his sleeve up and glanced at his watch. "Which we really must begin as quickly as possible because I've got a load of meetings today."

"See?" Zoe said. "He's a busy dude."

"Remember," Dr. Tenderfoot said. "The winner today will receive a prize bigger than they can even imagine."

"A million bucks split nine ways is still a ton of money," Wyatt said, hopeful.

"Who said it was a million bucks?" Gidget said, perking up. "Is that really what's on the table?"

"No," Zoe said. "Nobody knows what the prize is. Wyatt's just hoping, that's all."

"First up," Dr. Tenderfoot continued loudly, pointing one finger in the air. "Dante Sullivan and his team, if you please make your way to the center of the square at the middle of the room."

Dante stepped forward with his hands stuffed into his pockets. "I'm sorry," Dante said, embarrassed. "But I don't—"

I jumped forward, waving at Dr. Tenderfoot. "He's on our team now!" I said, cutting Dante off. "We thought we could do more if we teamed up!"

Dr. Tenderfoot's eyes squinted at me like he was studying some kind of bug. He took his monocle in his fingers and adjusted it over his eye. And then he pinched his mustache and rolled the end into a point.

"Interesting," Tenderfoot said. "So rather than have three teams compete today, we'll only have two?"

"Yep," I said.

Dr. Tenderfoot said nothing. He just stared at the center of the ring while twisting the end of his gentleman mustache. The microphone was picking up the breaths he took through his nostrils.

"What's he doing?" I asked.

"Thinking?" Zoe said. "I don't know."

Finally, the man with the mustache jolted back to reality. "Very well! The competition will be between *two* teams. I believe it makes things a little more interesting. We'll have a clear winner and a clear loser. The stakes are high, are they not?"

Dr. Tenderfoot spoke so strangely that nobody really knew how to answer his question. All he got was a confused mumble from the crowd.

"Then our first robot will come from Chance Cooper's team," Dr. Tenderfoot said.

"Uh," I said, raising my hand. "It's *Chase. Chase* Cooper."

"Of course," Dr. Tenderfoot said, nodding once at me. "My sincerest apologies, Chase Cooper."

"It's cool," I said, pushing our robot out to the center of the ring. "People make that mistake all the time." They didn't, but I didn't want Tenderfoot to feel stupid even though he probably wouldn't have.

When Hup-Hup was at the center of the ring, I waited for a second. I'm not sure why. Maybe it was because I knew our robot looked like junk after putting it back together. Or maybe it was because those moments before revealing anything were my favorite.

I always got chills at a movie theater right before flick starts. When the trailers end and the lights dim? Man, that's one of the best feelings in the world. It makes my heart race. Sometimes it ends up being better than the movie itself!

A moment later, I pulled the sheet off Hup-Hup, showing him to the entire school. Wyatt, Dante, and I managed to force the cow shell over the top of him, so he kind of looked okay, but if I told you a bunch of kindergarteners built it, you'd totes believe me.

Gidget snapped a selfie with Hup-Hup in the background.

Brayden and Slug gasped, shocked at how our robot looked.

Zoe and Faith raised their eyebrows at the same time.

Naomi let out a puff of air through her nose with a single laugh.

Dante was smiling like the robot was his BFF.

And Wyatt just looked angry.

Some kids giggled from the crowd. I ignored the few

147

comments that said the robot looked pathetic.

"Dr. Tenderfoot," I said boldly. "This is Hup-Hup. He's our robot, and we're proud of him. He might not be the prettiest thing, but he's *our* thing."

Dr. Tenderfoot's face was hard to read. He didn't look at the robot like it was a pile of junk. He looked at it like he was seriously interested. "Go on," he said. "Explain your choice in design."

I looked at Carlyle, and then back to Tenderfoot on the staircase. I was in front of the whole school. I didn't care to tell on Carlyle. It didn't matter because our robot was still in the game.

"We had some trouble about halfway through the project," I said. "This little guy's had a hard life for only being a week old."

"Doesn't matter," Tenderfoot said, half smiling. "What matters is that it performs the way you've built it to."

Nervously, I dropped to a knee and pressed my finger on the switch on the bottom of the robot. The last time we tested it, Hup-Hup worked perfectly, and that's including the change that Dante made at the last second.

I looked at the rest of my team, who all watched with shiny eyes. They were holding their breath, and then I realized I was doing the same thing. I sucked air into my lungs, and then slid the switch to the "on" position.

Nothing happened.

I stared at the robot, hoping that I could just *wish* it to life. Did robots have fairy godmothers? Pshhhh, who am I kidding? *Of course* robots had fairy godmothers!

"Don't do this to me, Hup-Hup," I said with my voice barely loud enough for even me to hear. "Don't embarrass me in front of my friends!"

I flipped the switch, but again, nothing happened.

Wyatt was standing in the corner, clenching his fists.

Dante looked like he was about to cry. I think he wanted the robot to work more than I did.

And then I heard the quiet buzzing sound again. The frayed wires! I put my hand through the hole and rolled the top of the wire between my fingers the same way that Dante had.

Just like that, Hup-Hup jumped back to life.

His little robot arm raised and lowered perfectly. His hand twisted in circles to look like he was waving at everyone in the library. And with Dante's addition, Hup-Hup slowly tilted back and forth while his body rotated.

Dante had a thin plastic pipe that pushed against the ground every time the hand rotated. Because the pipe was attached at an angle, it made the robot slowly spin in a circle.

The light bulb made the robot's eyes shine bright, and for a moment, I felt like it was actually a living thing.

HUP-HUP
...don't make fun, please.

Our team cheered loudly, raising their arms in the air victoriously. It wasn't because we thought we were going to win. It was because we got the dang thing to work.

Dante was the one celebrating the hardest. He was running back and forth, giving awkward high-fives to anyone who wanted one.

"Disqualified!" Carlyle shouted from his corner. "Their robot didn't even work at first! It wasn't finished in time! That prize should be ours!"

Dr. Tenderfoot raised his hand to tell Carlyle to quiet down. "It's alright," he said calmly. "All that matters is that it's doing what it was built to do. Some bumps in the road are inevitable, and can be a learning experience in and of themselves."

Carlyle stepped back, but didn't say anything else.

Dr. Tenderfoot clapped his hands towards my team. Everyone in the library followed his lead.

"Next up?" he said, waving at Carlyle's team.

Carlyle put his hand on his chin and cracked his neck.

The library was so quiet that you could hear the crunching sound.

He tapped once on the top of his covered robot, which BTW, was the size of a baby bear. The machine jostled, and then started moving toward the center of the ring all by itself!

"Interesting," Tenderfoot's voice whispered through the speaker system.

"Avast, ye landlubbers of Buchanan School!" Carlyle said as he walked with his moving robot. "Pay close attention because history is about to be made!"

"Dude," Brayden said. "That thing's moving by itself!"

Carlyle's covered robot stopped at the center of the ring and spun in a circle. "Allow me t'introduce ye to my team's project, Calypso!" He pulled the sheet off the machine they had been working on all week.

CALYPSO

It was amazing. The last time I saw their robot, it was still a pile of pieces on the floor of the science lab, and that was on Wednesday! In less than two days, they had created a

150

mechanical masterpiece.

The thing looked like it was from a sci-fi movie. It had a body with two arms and a head. Instead of legs, it had a metallic cover that I think was hiding wheels underneath. Little lights blinked on and off all over the head of the robot.

Calypso wobbled back and forth, making its way around the ring. As the robot circled around, it waved at the kids in the library. The gears inside squeaked as they moved.

Everyone was quiet, staring in awe of the machine Carlyle's team created.

"How in the heck did they build that thing?" Naomi asked.

"They're good, I guess," I said.

Carlyle walked proudly with his hands behind his back as he spoke. "Calypso is a state of the art robot who also obeys voice commands. Calypso, stop!"

The robot stopped in place, turning its head toward Carlyle.

"Calypso, bring me my book bag!" Carlyle commanded.

The little lights blipped on the robot's head, and then with a very mechanical voice, it said, *"As you wish, master."*

"Voice activated *and* can talk?" Brayden said. "Dude, we lose. That's it. Game over. We're all outta lives and outta continues."

Dante furrowed his eyebrows.

The whole library watched as Calypso wobbled over to Carlyle's bag, picked it up by the straps, and then wobbled it back to the pirate. When Calypso finished its mission, it swung back to face the crowd.

Everybody cheered. I even clapped my hands. I mean, it was seriously impressive.

"Calypso," Brayden said. "Come here and give me a high five!"

The robot turned toward my friend, and then said, *"Unknown user. Command not recognized."*

"Really?" Brayden laughed, along with a bunch of other kids in the crowd.

Calypso turned its head toward Carlyle, as if it was waiting for the pirate to tell it what to do. Carlyle squinted, and then waved his fingers slightly, signaling to the robot that he approved the high five.

The robot shook its head slowly.

"Whoa," I said under my breath. "That thing just refused to obey a command! This is it… this thing is the beginning of the robot apocalypse!"

Zoe must've heard me because she rolled her eyes. "*Nerd.*"

Carlyle stomped his foot down and stuck out his chest. "Calypso," he said sternly. "High five the student who asked for it!"

Calypso hesitated, but finally wobbled over to my friend.

Brayden held his open palm out.

"What if that thing high fives your hand right off your body?" I joked. "It *is* a robot that probably doesn't know its own strength!"

But Brayden didn't realize it was a joke. Just as Calypso swung its robot arm toward his hand, he pulled it back so the robot would miss.

Brayden's pine scented cologne wafted in the air around me. It was unusually strong, probably because he had just sprayed it only minutes ago.

Calypso stumbled forward, but caught itself. I could hear the robot whisper, "*Seriously?*"

Weird that a robot would have the ability to feel frustration.

And then the robot sneezed. "*Waaa-choo!*"

Even Dr. Tenderfoot raised an eyebrow.

"Whoa," Slug said like the dude from that movie about a time travelling phone booth and an excellent adventure. "Any robot that sneezes is too real for me."

"Wait a second," I said, watching the robot as it wobbled back to Carlyle. I turned to Brayden. "Gimme your perfume!"

Brayden pulled the small bottle from his book bag. "It's *cologne.*"

"Whatever!" I said, taking the bottle from my friend. I raised the cologne and pointed it at Calypso, but the robot was too far away.

So, without thinking, I ran toward the robot, spraying the cologne as I circled around it.

"*What're you doing?*" Carlyle shouted.

"Young man!" Dr. Tenderfoot boomed from the staircase. "This rude interruption will cost you the competition! You *will* be disqualified if you don't exit the

152

ring!"

Even Principal Davis shouted at me from the edge of the library. "Chase, get over here, right now! This is extremely inappropriate!"

I heard Zoe scold me from somewhere, but I couldn't see her since I was still running circles and spraying Calypso.

Kids were "*booing*" me from the crowd, yelling about how lame of a loser I was.

But all the shouts stopped when Calypso sneezed again. "*Waaa-choo!*"

All heads turned toward Carlyle's robot.

Finally, I stopped. Through the fog of pine scented cologne, I watched as Calypso tried to wobble away from the manly musk of lumberjacks.

But the robot couldn't move fast enough. The cloud of cologne drifted slowly around it. And then the sneezing fit started. Over and over, Calypso sneezed. And each sneeze grew stronger than the last.

"No!" Carlyle said. "You can't get my robot wet! That's cheating! She'll short circuit! I mean, *it'll* short circuit!"

With a final, super strong sneeze, Calypso bent forward, sending its head flying through the ring until it stopped at the bottom of the staircase.

Dr. Tenderfoot stared at the robot's head on the floor in front of him. When he looked back at Calypso, he pressed his lips to one side of his face and shook his head slowly.

Calypso was still at the center of the ring as the school stared at the strange sight before their eyes. The robot's body was still intact, blinking with colorful lights. On top of the robot's shoulders was another head, but it wasn't a robot.

It was Olivia Jones. Calypso wasn't a functioning robot at all. It was Olivia dressed in a robot costume.

Slug gasped. "Olivia's been turned into a machine!"

His twin sister sighed heavily, shaking her head. "It's a costume, dude…"

Slug's eyebrows furrowed a bit as he breathed through his mouth. "Oh, that makes more sense."

Olivia sat in the center of the ring, shocked. But her

frown flipped into a smile because what else can you do when you get caught cheating? And then she sneezed one final time. It was strong enough that she tipped over and fell to the ground.

The rest of the robot costume peeled apart. Olivia had been moving the robot using the tricycle I had seen in the science lab.

Dr. Tenderfoot didn't waste a second with accusations or speeches about cheating and disappointment. He pointed at Hup-Hup, and spoke loudly. "We have our winner, ladies and gentlemen!"

"Why couldn't you hold your sneezes back?" Carlyle said angrily.

Olivia was rolling around on the floor, stuck in her robot costume. "Because I'm human! He sprayed that garbage all over and made me sneeze like crazy! Gag! So gross!"

"Well, thanks to your dumb allergies, we lost!" Carlyle said.

"Don't you dare blame me for this!" Olivia said. "This was *your* idea! And because of that, we're out a million bucks!"

"A million dollars?" Dr. Tenderfoot said into the mic. "There's no way that ridiculous costume cost a million dollars to make."

Carlyle glared at the man with the mustache. "No, ye scurvy infested fool! The million dollar prize for th'winner of the competition!"

The crowd fell silent.

"*Scurvy infested fool?*" Dr. Tenderfoot repeated.

"Oh, snap!" Slug whispered. "Carlyle's finished!"

"Whoopsies," Carlyle said.

Tenderfoot didn't say anything else to Carlyle after that. He just waved his hand at Principal Davis, who understood immediately that he was supposed to remove the pirate from the room.

Olivia wiggled around to free herself from her costume. It took nearly a minute and everyone watched in awkward silence. It was weird.

Finally, she managed to get it off. She stood at the center of the ring, still sneezing every few seconds. Then she looked at Wyatt with soft eyes. "Hey, babe! Looks like we won, huh?"

Wyatt scrunched his nose, shocked that Olivia was trying to switch sides again, but he didn't have time to respond. Principal Davis shouted for her to get to the library doors.

A bunch of students covered their mouths and said, "*Ohhhhhhhhhh!*"

Dr. Tenderfoot had other places to be, so he continued quickly. "Would the leader of the *real* winning team please come to the staircase?"

Zoe patted my back, nudging me forward. It was a little embarrassing, but in a good way.

But as I started for the staircase, Wyatt grabbed my elbow, pulling me back. He peeled out past me, running at full speed until he got to Dr. Tenderfoot's side, halfway up the stairs.

"What's he..." I said.

Wyatt pointed his fingers at the crowd, and then grabbed the microphone from Dr. Tenderfoot, but not without a small struggle from the man with a mustache. I don't think Dr. Tenderfoot wanted to let Wyatt speak, but he didn't have a choice once Wyatt ripped the mic from his hands.

Naomi stood next to me, and together we watched as

Wyatt did his usual "Wyatt" thing.

"Thank you!" he said into the microphone. "Thank you so very much! It's been a long journey, but I did it! With the help of my team, of course! But it was mostly me, the team captain, and yeah, I'm here to claim the prize on behalf of the rest of the team!"

"Oh, really?" Dr. Tenderfoot asked.

"Yup," Wyatt said. "Lay that million bucks on me, Dr. Tenderbutt. I'm ready to be so rich that I can *literally* buy happiness!"

The man with the mustache looked confused. "Who said *anything* about a million dollars?"

"Uhhhh," Wyatt said, thinking. "It's *not* a million bucks? That's fine. Whatever the prize is, I'll go ahead and take it now. It's still a prize greater than I can imagine!"

"It is, young man," Dr. Tenderfoot said. "The prize is…"

Tenderfoot paused for effect. All the kids in the library

fell silent, waiting for him to drop the bomb.

Even Wyatt was staring slack-jawed at the man with the mustache. His eyes grew wider with every nanosecond that passed.

"Victory," Dr. Tenderfoot said with a calm voice.

Wyatt dropped the mic, but it was so quiet that everyone could still hear his voice. "Victory?"

"*Victory* is its own reward," Tenderfoot said, pinching the end of his mustache.

"That's nothing," Wyatt said. "That's not something greater than I can imagine! Something greater than I can imagine would be a trip to Saturn! It'd be my own island in the Bahamas! *It'd be a million bucks!*"

"Whoa," I said, blown away by the fact that I wasn't bothered by what Dr. Tenderfoot said.

"The machine your team built won the competition," Dr. Tenderfoot explained. "You may not think much of it, but look at the other two teams… one cheated, and one completely disappeared. Only *your* robot remains in the ring. This competition *wasn't* as easy as everyone thought it would be, was it?"

Wyatt didn't answer, but I don't think he heard the question.

"So the reward for the winning team," Dr. Tenderfoot said again, "…is *victory*. You've overcome hurdles to get here. Imagine what else you could do if you tried."

"Laaaaame," Wyatt sang, but he wasn't one to miss an opportunity to gloat. He put his hands in the air and waved victoriously.

The applause from the crowd was slow and awkward at first, but eventually grew into a mighty roar that sounded like it was going to bring down the house. Kids will cheer for anything if enough people are cheering with them.

And Wyatt ate it up. He put his hands together over his head and pumped them up and down. *This* was his reward. *This* was his victory.

Naomi nudged me with her elbow. "You can stop this, you know. *You're* the team captain. It should be *you* up there."

"I know," I said, watching Wyatt. "But it doesn't bother me."

"I knew it wouldn't," Naomi smiled.

Everyone was cheering loud enough that nobody could

hear our conversation.

"Just because Carlyle and Olivia were busted doesn't mean the red and green ninjas are finished," I explained. "They'll be back, and I think I'm going to need Wyatt's help. If I go up there and call him out, then he'll just get angry with me. Besides, look at him. I think he needs this more than I do."

Naomi watched Wyatt as he continued to overdo it on the staircase. He had started flexing his arms and posing like a body builder.

I knew I wasn't going to get in the middle of a family feud between Wyatt and Carlyle, but I couldn't be sure *they* would keep me out of it.

"But you're letting him get away with a lie," Naomi said.

"Nah, I don't see it like that," I said. "Wyatt might, but I don't. We couldn't have built Hup-Hup without his help. It doesn't make a different whether it's him or me up there, and as the *actual* team leader, I'm okay with him taking credit. It's not a battle worth fighting. And right now, with what Carlyle's done, I think we'll need as many people on our side as we can get. I have this awful feeling that a war is coming."

"So you're cool with all this?" Naomi asked me. "You're forgiving him?"

I thought about it for a second. "Yeah," I said without a doubt. "Isn't that the risk you take whenever you forgive anyone? Either they've changed, or they'll burn you again."

"I suppose," Naomi said. "It's never as black and white as that though. I don't even think this is about Wyatt, is it?"

I couldn't help but let a smile show. "If I *didn't* let him on our team, then I'd be on the path to the dark side."

"Nerd," Naomi rolled her eyes. "*Such* a nerd."

I LOL'd.

Naomi slugged me in the arm. The same spot that Zoe and Faith kept hitting. Great. Now *Naomi* was in on it too.

Wyatt was still on the staircase handing out high-fives like he invented them. Dr. Tenderfoot wasn't next to him anymore.

In fact, he was next to me.

"Impressive work, Chase Cooper," Dr. Tenderfoot said.

"Thanks," I said, and then waved to the rest of my friends behind me. "But it couldn't have happened without the team."

"Well, they had a good leader," Tenderfoot said. The monocle on his eye reflected the library lights.

I bit my lip, glancing at Wyatt. "Yeah, I guess," I said.

Dr. Tenderfoot paused. "I'm not talking about that showboat... I'm talking about you."

I was speechless, even though my mouth was trying to say something.

"Don't make a thing of it, young man," Dr. Tenderfoot said. "That's what makes you, *you*. You don't need all the..." He waved his hands at Wyatt and made an annoyed face. "*Show*."

"Thanks," was all I was going to say, but then I remembered the mystery about the blank slips of paper from the beginning of the week. "Hey, about the names you picked out of your hat..."

"What about them?" Tenderfoot's mustache twitched.

"All the slips of paper were blank," I said.

Dr. Tenderfoot took his monocle between his fingers and let it dangle in front of my face. My reflection was wonky on the lens.

I took it carefully, not wanting to accidentally break it. And the man with the mustache took a slip of paper from his tuxedo pocket, holding it up to me. It was white.

Completely blank.

"Look through the glass, m'boy," Dr. Tenderfoot said with a hint of excitement in his voice.

I brought the monocle to my eye and looked at the slip of paper he was holding. It wasn't blank anymore. It was a list of meetings he needed to be at that day.

"It's, like, invisible ink or something?" I asked.

"Something like that," Dr. Tenderfoot said. "Your cousin printed everyone's name, but I had them *reprinted*, because, well... why not? Invisible ink is fun, isn't it?"

For the first time, I wasn't intimidated by Dr. Tenderfoot. He might've been a prestigious inventor, but he was still a giddy kid at heart.

The monocle was a lot heavier than I would've guessed. I held it in my open palm to give it back to the man with the mustache.

When I looked up... Dr. Ashley Tenderfoot was gone.

But it was because I looked in the wrong direction. He was actually rushing for the library doors.

"Wait," I shouted, but he knew what I was going to say.

"Keep it!" he said over his shoulder. "I got a million of them!"

"Huh," I said, inspecting the monocle once more before stuffing it into my front pocket.

My friends surrounded me, almost tackling me to the ground. Everyone was there – Zoe, Faith, Gidget, Slug, Brayden, Naomi, and Dante. They were excited, celebrating the fact that we won the competition even though there wasn't a prize.

We spent the rest of the morning playing with Hup-Hup and showing everyone how we made him work.

Wyatt was still taking all the credit, but it didn't bother me. Really, it didn't.

Was he still the bad guy? Maybe. Maybe not. I think he was stuck somewhere in the middle. I wasn't sure what his endgame was, but I knew it was *something*. And with Wyatt's history, it was something *big*.

But we had a deal. We'd leave each other alone after the holiday ninjas had been dealt with. I could only hope he'd keep up his end of the bargain.

Plus, with the threat of the holiday ninjas in the shadows, I'd rather have Wyatt in a place where I could see him, and there in the library, the entire school could see him.

No matter how shady he was though, he had still helped the team build Hup-Hup.

It wasn't much, but it was a start.

The rest of Team Cooper surrounded me, lining up for a photo.

Melvin, one of the school reporters, held up a camera and said, "Yearbook photo on three! One… two…"

"Chase," Naomi said from the end of the group.

I looked to see what she wanted, but she didn't say anything. She was making an ugly face at me.

Without thinking, I made my best ugly face back at her.

Naomi smiled as her head snapped back toward the camera, which flashed.

Sighing, I rolled my head back because I knew exactly what happened. Naomi just proved her point and the yearbook was going to have evidence of it.

Ugly faces *were* contagious.

**BONUS FACT ABOUT THIS BOOK:**
THIS IS A PICTURE OF MY SON, PARKER,
AND ME. CHASE'S FUNNY FACE IS BASED
ON THIS FUNNY FACE THAT PARKER MAKES.
HE DOES THIS IN EVERY PICTURE BECAUSE
HE KNOWS IT MAKES PEOPLE LAUGH.
EVERY. SINGLE. PICTURE.

*Stories – what an incredible way to open one's mind to a fantastic world of adventure. It's my hope that this story has inspired you in some way, lighting a fire that maybe you didn't know you had. Keep that flame burning no matter what. It represents your sense of adventure and creativity, and that's something nobody can take from you. Thanks for reading! If you enjoyed this book, I ask that you help spread the word by sharing it or leaving an honest review!*

*- Marcus*
*m@MarcusEmerson.com*

**Marcus Emerson** is the author of several highly imaginative children's books including the 6th Grade Ninja series, Secret Agent 6th Grader, and Totes Sweet Hero. His goal is to create children's books that are engaging, funny, and inspirational for kids of all ages - even the adults who secretly never grew up.

Marcus Emerson is currently having the time of his life with his beautiful wife and their four amazing children. He still dreams of becoming an astronaut someday and walking on Mars.

Made in the USA
Middletown, DE
26 June 2015